Judi Curtin

Stand By Me

THE O'BRIEN PRESS
DUBLIN

First published 2017 by
The O'Brien Press Ltd,
12 Terenure Road East, Rathgar,
Dublin 6, D06 HD27 Ireland.
Tel: +353 1 4923333; Fax: +353 1 4922777
E-mail: books@obrien.ie.
Website: www.obrien.ie
The O'Brien Press is a member of Publishing Ireland

ISBN: 978-1-84717-964-7

1 3 5 7 8 6 4 2
17 19 21 20 18

Cover and internal illustrations by Rachel Corcoran.
Printed and bound by Norhaven Paperback A/S, Denmark.

The paper in this book is produced using pulp from managed forests.

Published in

DUBLIN

UNESCO
City of Literature

Chapter One

'**B**ye, Mollikins. Talk soon. Love you.'

'Dad? Are you ever going to stop calling me Mollikins?'

'No.'

'Oh, OK. Bye, Dad, love you too.'

I clicked off the call, and lay down on my bed. Face-timing my dad is always really nice, but I can't help feeling sad when it's time to say goodbye. I hadn't seen Dad for ages and ages, and even though I'm often mad at him, I really, really miss him. The first tears were coming to my eyes when Beth flung the door open and threw herself on to the bed beside me.

'You've been talking to your dad, haven't you?' she said.

'How do you know?'

'Wild guess,' she said pointing to my eyes. 'I'm

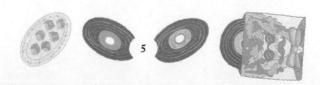

sorry, Moll – it sucks having your dad living so far away.'

It was nice of her to say that. She was right, it *did* suck having my dad so far away, but her mum is dead, and that has to be a million times worse.

Beth hugged me and then she jumped up. 'Come on,' she said. 'I've got some pocket-money left. How about I buy us both ice-creams?'

'Sounds like an excellent plan. Let's go.'

* * *

We were nearly at the shop when we heard the sound of cheeps and quacks coming along behind us. It was so loud – it was like a riot in a bird sanctuary. 'OMG! What on earth is that noise?' said Beth By the time we turned around, the noise was right next to us.

'Hi, girls,' said a familiar voice over the quacking noise. 'How nice to see you.'

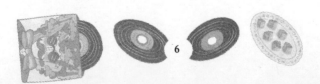

'Graham!' said Beth. '*What* are you doing? I didn't even know you were back from your holidays.'

'I just got back last night – it was a wonderful trip – one of the best ever.'

Graham smiled at us and tossed his head to get his long hair out of his huge dark-brown eyes. He's tall and skinny and he was wearing ripped denim jeans, and a t-shirt with a picture of his favourite rock band. He was carrying a huge shopping bag – not that unusual really, except that the bag was wriggling and shaking like it was alive.

'Please don't say that awful noise is coming from your bag,' said Beth.

'*What* have you got inside there?' I asked.

'Oh, it's just a mother duck and her babies,' Graham said casually, like the bag held nothing more special than a loaf of bread and a carton of milk. 'They were lost on a very busy road, so I rescued them from certain death, and now I'm bringing them to the pond where they'll be safe.'

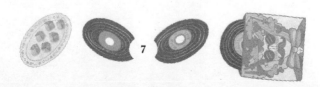

'That's really nice of you,' said Beth, laughing. 'But what is it about you? How come you always show up when weird stuff happens?'

'I wasn't the only one who showed up,' he said. 'Lots of people were there.'

'And why didn't they help?' I asked.

'Who knows?' said Graham. 'Some of them ignored the ducks, but others stopped to take photos and then left the poor creatures to their fate.'

'That's really mean,' I said.

'Can Molly and I come to the pond with you?' asked Beth.

'Of course you can,' said Graham. 'We can rescue this little family together.'

* * *

At the pond, Graham put down the bag and the mother duck tumbled out, shaking herself and ruffling her feathers. She quacked loudly, and five

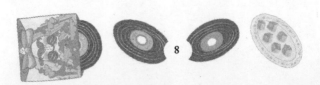

totally adorable, fluffy little ducklings rolled out of the bag and waddled out after her. Then all six flung themselves into the water, like they'd never seen anything so amazing. The mother looked back at us for a second and quacked.

'She's thanking you, Graham,' said Beth. 'She knows you saved her family.'

Then the mother and her babies swam off, and seconds later they were hidden in the clumps of weeds in the middle of the pond.

'Molly and I were on our way to the shop to buy ice-cream,' said Beth. 'Do you want to come?'

'Sure,' said Graham. 'But first there's something I have to do – I always do it when I come to this park.'

I couldn't help feeling excited. I don't know what the opposite of boring is, but whatever it is, that's the best word to describe Graham.

We followed him up the short steep hill to where the monument is. Then he stood for a second letting the wind blow through his long hair.

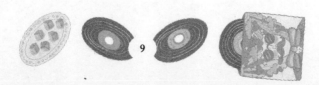

'Now what do we do?' asked Beth.

'This!' said Graham, as he flung himself down on the grass and rolled down to the bottom of the hill.

I looked at Beth for a second.

Weren't we too old for rolling down hills?

What would Mum say if we got grass stains on our clothes?

What if there was dog poo – which had to be the grossest thing in the world?

But then I looked at Graham, who was sitting on the grass below us, breathless and laughing like a little kid.

'Last one down's an idiot,' I said, and then Beth and I rolled to the bottom of the hill where we lay on our backs and looked at the sky and laughed till we felt sick.

'You know you're crazy, right, Graham?' said Beth when she got her breath back.

'Thank you, Beth,' said Graham. 'That's the nicest thing anyone's said to me all day.'

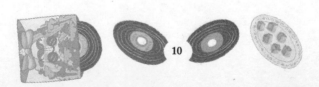

Beth was right. Graham *is* crazy. He's the craziest nearly-seventy-year-old I've ever met.

* * *

Graham is Beth's dad's uncle. He always wears jeans and t-shirts and when it's cold he puts on weird jumpers he buys in a village at the top of a mountain no one's ever heard of, somewhere in South America. He knows about nature and art and music and films and books and sport. He travels the world for months at a time, and we never know when he's going to show up at his tiny little house not far from where we live. He's the most fun person I've ever known.

* * *

On the way to the shop, we passed the animal shelter.

'Let's go in for just one second,' begged Graham, like he was the kid and Beth and I were the adults. 'I

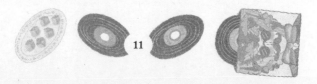

love to see the puppies and kittens.'

So we followed him inside and for twenty minutes we petted and stroked every kind of furry creature we could see.

On the way out we passed a poster saying *'ALL DONATIONS WELCOME – PLEASE SUPPORT OUR WORK.'* Graham dug around in his pockets and put all the money he could find into the collection bucket.

'Hey, Molly,' said Beth. 'How badly do you want the ice-cream I promised you?'

I actually wanted it fairly badly – in my head I'd already chosen the chocolate brownie and salted caramel flavours. I could already almost taste the creamy coldness and the squishy caramel pieces on my tongue – but then I saw the huge eyes of a darling little puppy staring at me from the poster and I shook my head.

'Who needs ice-cream?' I said, and then I helped Beth to put the coins through the slot.

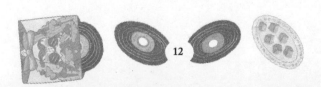

That's the weird thing about Graham – he's wild and crazy and funny, but there's also something else about him – just being with him makes you want to be a better person.

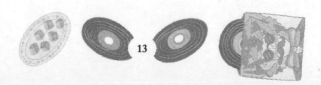

Chapter Two

'That carrot cake is totally delicious, Charlotte,' said Beth after lunch. 'Thanks so much for making it.'

'Anything for you, my little pet,' said Mum. 'I know it's your favourite.'

I rolled my eyes. I know Mum loves me more than she will ever love Beth, but things changed when Beth and her dad came to live with us. Since then, Mum and Beth have been getting closer and closer, and sometimes I can't help feeling a small bit jealous. Sometimes, when Mum makes carrot cake instead of my favourite chocolate one, I feel like she's choosing Beth over me. (I know that's unreasonable, but I can't help it – I'm just a kid.)

'Anyone for a second slice?' asked Beth's dad, Jim. 'There's lots left.'

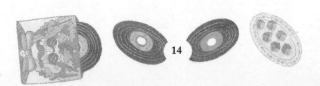

We all shook our heads – the slices he'd served first time around were ginormous, and even a carrot cake fiend like Beth couldn't force down another crumb.

'I know!' I said. 'Why don't Beth and I bring a slice over to Graham? He loves carrot cake too – must be a family thing.'

'You're not just trying to get out of doing the washing up?' said Mum, and I felt like jumping up and down and stamping my foot like a toddler in a tantrum. I was trying to do a nice thing, so why did Mum have to think I was being selfish?

Maybe Mum noticed smoke coming out of my ears or something, because she leaned over and hugged me. 'That's a very kind thought, Molly,' she said. 'You're a sweet girl. Off you go.'

* * *

'You darling girls,' said Graham when he opened the front door. 'And carrot cake too – all my dreams have

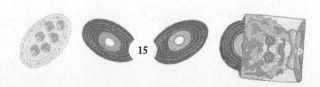

just come true!'

Beth and I followed Graham into the living room at the back of his house.

'I'll get us some tea,' he said. 'You two sit down and make yourselves comfortable.'

I tried not to smile. There were lots of places to sit in Graham's living room, but none of them looked very comfortable. There was an ancient lumpy old couch, two wobbly stools, and an armchair that would've been quite nice except for the rusty springs sticking out all over. I chose the safest-looking stool, and Beth sat on the edge of the couch.

While Graham clattered about in the kitchen, I looked around the room. The shelves in the corner were piled up with books, and there were more piles of books on the floor and the window-sill. The fireplace and the table were packed with colourful sculptures from all over the world. In the middle of the floor was a huge open box, and we could see more ornaments poking out of the

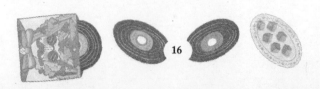

shredded-paper packing.

'I guess Graham's been treasure hunting again,' said Beth looking at the box. 'Where's he even going to put all these new things?'

'No idea,' I said. 'I totally love this house, but there's one thing I've always wondered about.'

'What?'

'The house is stuffed with stuff, but there are no pictures or photographs anywhere on the walls.'

'Graham's house has always been like this – even when I was a tiny kid – I don't even notice it any more.'

'I know, but don't you think it's really weird that—?'

'Really weird that what?' asked Graham. He was wearing soft leather sandals and I hadn't heard him come in.

'Oh ... er ... nothing,' I said, embarrassed. 'Here, let me help you with the tray.'

I jumped up and moved a huge pile of books, so he could put the tray on the table. Then I sat down again

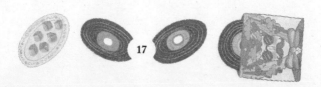

and Graham handed out the drinks. Tea isn't usually the most exciting drink in the world, but in Graham's house, nothing is ever very usual. The tea was served in tall, narrow, golden-coloured glasses. Instead of a boring old teabag, each glass had a flower floating in it. While I watched, the flowers expanded in the hot water – it was like watching a slow-motion nature film.

'OMG!' said Beth. 'That's the coolest thing ever. Are they real flowers?'

'Of course,' said Graham. 'It's called blooming tea. I picked it up last time I was in China. My good friend Chang makes it. Why don't you try it and tell me what you think?'

I sipped my tea. 'Wow!' I said. 'It tastes like strawberry and peach and ...'

'It's like drinking a fruit bowl,' said Beth. 'It's the best thing I've ever, ever tasted.'

Just then the doorbell rang.

'That'll be my friend,' said Graham, jumping up

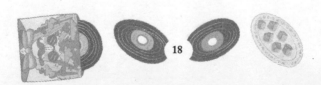

from his wobbly stool and running out to the hall. 'He said he might drop by today.'

Beth raised her eyebrows and I knew what she was trying to tell me. Graham has lots and lots of friends and some of them are ... interesting.

A second later, Graham was back. 'Girls,' he said. 'Meet my friend, Charlie.'

Mum's forever telling me not to be judgmental, and I really try, but ...

Beth recovered quicker than I did, as she stood up and said 'hi' to the homeless man who sleeps at the back of the shopping centre.

'Er ... hi, Charlie,' I said trying not to think of the last time I saw him, digging around in the bins behind the supermarket. 'It's nice to meet you.'

'Hello,' said Charlie in a quiet voice. I felt sorry that he had to sit on the armchair with the sticky-out springs, but maybe that seemed comfortable to a man whose bed is a dirty sleeping-bag and a few sheets of cardboard?

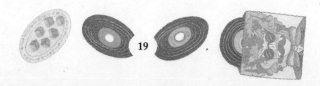

Graham brought some tea for Charlie, and gave him most of the carrot cake, and Charlie kept saying 'thank you' over and over again until it started to make me feel sad.

* * *

For a bit it was totally awkward, but then, while we sipped our tea, Graham told us about his latest travels, which included visits to Morocco and Tunisia and Greece. Soon I had a pain in my side from laughing. Charlie seemed kind of shy and he didn't say a whole lot, but he laughed too.

'You're so funny, Graham,' I said. 'I think you could make a trip to the dentist sound interesting.'

'You're too kind,' said Graham. 'But anyway, enough about me – tell me what's going on for you two girls. How is school?'

'School's OK, I guess,' I said. 'Except for the maths project and the history essay I haven't even

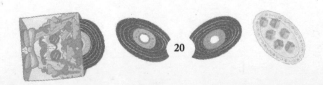

started yet.'

'But you and I should be *especially* good at history, Molly,' said Beth.

'Why is that?' asked Graham.

I made a face at Beth. I knew she was thinking of our time-travelling trips to the past – and they were supposed to be top secret.

'Oh, no real reason,' said Beth, looking guilty.

'Oh, well, don't worry about it,' said Graham. 'School is greatly over-rated, in my opinion.'

I giggled, wondering what my parents would have to say about that.

We talked for another while, and then Beth jumped up.

'Molly and I have to go. You know how crazy my dad gets when we're late.'

Charlie stood up too. 'It think it's time for me to ...'

'Won't you stay and have some stew, Charlie?' said Graham. 'I made too much as usual.'

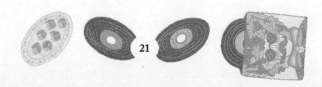

'That's so kind of you,' said Charlie in a hoarse voice.

'Er ... goodbye, Charlie,' I said. 'It was really nice to meet you.' And then I looked away quickly because I was fairly sure he was getting ready to cry.

Graham walked us to the door.

Beth hugged him. 'You're a very kind man,' she said.

'Not at all. Not at all,' he said, embarrassed. Then he changed the subject quickly. 'Look at what arrived while I was away,' he said, pointing at a huge pile of unopened letters on the hall table. 'Maybe I should just chuck the whole lot in the fire and pretend I never got them.'

'No way,' said Beth. 'You have to open them. There could be amazing good news in one of them, and if you burn them you'll never know.'

'Yeah,' I said. 'Maybe one of those letters is telling you that you won a million euros or something.'

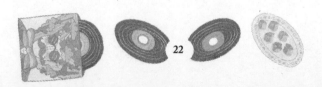

'I suppose you're right,' said Graham, shoving the letters into a box under the table. 'I promise I'll deal with them – some other day.'

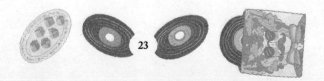

Chapter Three

The next night, Beth's dad, Jim, made pasta for dinner. He makes really great pasta, so no one talked much until our plates were almost cleared.

'We should ask Graham to join us for dinner tomorrow evening,' said Mum as we were scraping up the last of the totally delicious, creamy sauce.

'Yay!' said Beth and I together. Dinner's always much more fun when Graham's around.

Then I remembered something. 'Do you know why Graham hasn't got any pictures on the walls in his house, Jim? There's not a single picture or photograph or poster – or anything.'

Jim shook his head. 'No idea. I've been visiting Graham's house since I was a little boy, and it's always been like that. I even asked my dad about it once – he was Graham's brother, you know.'

'And what did your dad say?' asked Beth.

'He didn't have a clue either. I wanted to ask Graham if there was a reason, but my dad wouldn't let me.'

'Why?' I asked.

Jim shook his head. 'My dad wouldn't say, but once, when I was a bit older, when Graham was away on his travels, Dad talked a bit more about him.'

'What did he say?' asked Mum.

'He said that Graham was much younger than him, but that when he was little, he was a cute, normal kid – always laughing and running around. He said he was a bit of a daredevil.'

'That sounds about right,' I said, remembering him rolling down the hill, and not caring that everyone in the park was staring at him.

'Graham's always had a wild streak,' said Jim. 'But my dad did say one other thing though.'

'What?' asked Mum.

'My dad went to work in London when Graham

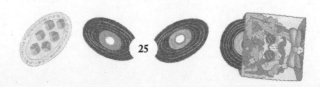

was very young – and he said that at the end of one summer, when Dad came home on holidays, Graham was like a different boy.'

'Different how?' I asked.

'My dad couldn't really explain it – even many years later he seemed mystified. He said Graham was unusually quiet that September, and a bit removed from the world – it was almost like a little part of his younger brother had died.'

'What had happened to him?' asked Mum.

'That's the strange thing – as far as the family knew, nothing at all had happened.'

'And what did Graham say about it?' asked Beth.

'I'm not sure anyone asked him,' said Jim. 'Things were different back then. It would've been ... the late 1950's or ... actually I remember now – my dad said it was 1960 – his last year in London. People didn't talk about their feelings in those days – there was lots left unsaid. I think people thought that if they didn't talk about their problems they might magically disappear.'

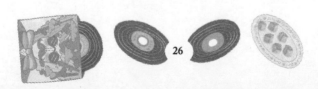

'As if that was a good strategy for mental health!' said Mum.

'And what happened after that?' I asked.

'Well, nothing really,' said Jim. 'Next time my dad came home, Graham seemed to have snapped out of it. He might not have been exactly back to normal, but he didn't seem quite as sad as before, and, well you know how it is – life goes on.'

'You all know I'm very fond of Graham,' said Mum. 'But if you ask me, there's something strange about a man who travels abroad as much as he does.'

'Muuum!' I said. 'That's so stupid. I'd go on holidays every single day if I could. I'd go to Africa and Australia and—'

I know you would,' said Mum smiling. 'But Graham's a grown-up and grown-ups don't do things like that. It's almost like Graham's running away.'

'Running away from what?' I asked.

'You mean like a murder or something?' asked Beth, giggling.

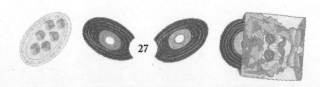

I giggled too. 'Graham wouldn't hurt a fly – literally,' I said. 'He so wasn't happy when I tried to kill one with a newspaper last summer.'

'And he saved those poor ducks from being knocked down,' said Beth.

'And remember when there was a mouse in his kitchen last winter?' I said. 'Graham gave it a big lump of cheese and then set it free in the garden.'

Everyone laughed.

'You know perfectly well I didn't mean that Graham committed a crime,' said Mum. 'It's more like there's something he can't face up to. It's as if trekking halfway across the world is easier for him than dealing with stuff that's going on in his head.'

'That's interesting,' I said. 'And maybe it's true – but it still doesn't explain why the walls of Graham's house are completely bare.'

'It's a mystery, all right,' said Mum.

'And some mysteries will never be solved,' said Jim. 'Like the mystery of who here is ready for a

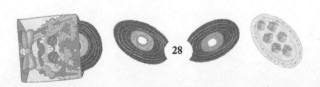

chocolate brownie?'

Jim's jokes are usually pretty lame, but his brownies are amazing, so I resisted rolling my eyes, and raced Beth to the fridge to get out the dessert.

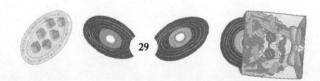

Chapter Four

'We've got so much homework,' I wailed, as we walked slowly home from school a few days later. 'It's child cruelty. There should be a law against it.'

'You're such a drama queen,' said Beth.

'You sound like my mother.'

She made a face. 'I hope you're joking. I love your mum – but I so don't want to be her. Anyway, maybe you don't have to face your homework this very minute. Let's call to Graham's place and see if he's started planning his next trip yet.'

Visiting Graham sounded like a whole lot more fun than studying for a geography test, so I texted Mum to tell her we'd be late, and then walked a bit faster, ready to be entertained by our old friend.

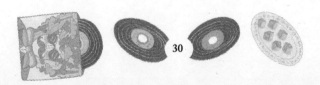

* * *

'My two favourite girls in the whole world! Do come in and tell me about your day.'

Graham was smiling as usual, but as Beth and I followed him into the living room, I knew something was different. It was like his smile was fake and forced – as if really he was crying inside. I looked at Beth and I could see by her face that she felt it too.

I'd been hoping for one of his delicious blooming teas, but Graham didn't even glance towards the kitchen. He sat on one of the wobbly stools and looked really miserable. For the first time ever, he looked like an old man.

On the table beside him was an open letter, and next to that was an old photo album.

What was going on? I felt shy and embarrassed. Graham always cheers us up and makes us laugh – and I had no idea what to say to this new, quiet man.

'Er ... Are you OK, Graham?' asked Beth.

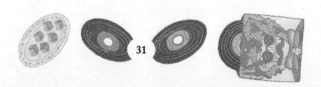

'Why wouldn't I be OK?' He wasn't answering her question, which is never a good sign.

'You just seem a bit ... sad,' said Beth.

'Oh, I'll be fine,' said Graham. 'Don't you worry about me. Now, any news from your lovely world?'

'Well, our teacher's a crazy work-fiend and she's given us tons of homework and ...'

But then I stopped myself. I remembered what Jim had said about people long ago bottling up their problems. 'Er ... Beth and I are good listeners,' I said.

'And?' Graham looked at me, and I couldn't tell if he was angry. Did he think I was just some nosy kid trying to push my way into his private business?

I looked desperately at Beth, hoping she could help me. Instead she picked up the photo album and opened it. On the first page there was a big old black and white photo of a boy and a girl – both aged about twelve or thirteen. They were sitting on a rug, having a picnic, with proper plates and cutlery, and very fancy looking sandwiches.

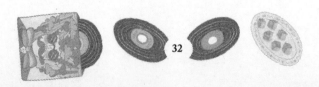

'Who's this?' she asked.

For a long time, Graham didn't say anything – and it was totally awkward.

Then he shook his head, and it was like he'd made a big decision.

'That's me,' he said, pointing at the boy.

I forgot about the awkwardness of the moment, as I struggled to see Graham in the picture of the boy with the slicked-back hair and the cheeky grin. Then I suddenly got it, as I looked at the huge dark eyes.

'OMG!' I said. 'It really is you. You're adorable, Graham. The girls must have loved you.'

'They still do, actually,' he said. 'I'm not quite past it yet.' For a second he looked normal and happy, before his smile faded away again.

Then Beth pointed at the girl, who was also grinning madly. She had curly hair, and a huge spotty bow on the top of her head. She had pointy-edged glasses that looked like she was wearing them for a bet. She looked cheeky and fun – the kind of girl

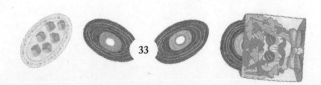

you'd want to be friends with.

'And who's this girl?' asked Beth.

This time the silence dragged on and on and on until it was almost unbearable. I could hear the ticking of Graham's old watch, and the sound of kids playing outside. I started to wish I was at home studying my geography, or emptying the dishwasher or doing something totally fun like that.

And then Graham leaned over the photograph. He touched the picture, like it was the most precious thing he had ever owned.

'That,' he said. 'Is Jeanie Cottrell-Herbert.'

'Oooh, sounds posh,' I said.

'Jeanie's family was undoubtedly posh,' said Graham. 'And I'm sad to say her parents didn't like me at all.'

'Why?' I asked, feeling mad for him. How could anyone not like Graham? He's a total sweetheart.

'Oh, I don't think it was me exactly that they objected to – it was more that I wasn't the son of one

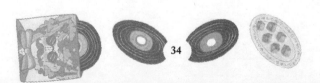

of their posh friends. They thought I was too rough for their precious girl – but Jeanie didn't care about things like that. She was just very sweet. That girl had a laugh that could make the birds sing – when she laughed, you wanted to join in with her, no matter how bad you were feeling.'

'OMG!' said Beth. 'Now I get it. Jeanie was your first girlfriend, wasn't she?'

'No, no, it was nothing like that,' said Graham. 'We were young and innocent. We simply spent lots of time together – whole summers long.'

'Doing what?' asked Beth who clearly wasn't convinced by the whole 'just friends' thing.

'Well, one year we danced a lot,' said Graham.

'Danced?' I said. 'You mean like ballroom dancing or something?'

'No,' he said. 'I'm not quite that ancient, you know. It was 1960 – pop music had just been born.'

OMG, 1960, wasn't that the year that Jim said Graham began acting strangely?

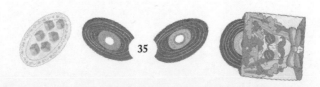

Beth musn't have noticed. 'Did you love The Beatles back then?' she asked.

'No,' said Graham again. 'The Beatles may well have existed, but we'd never heard of them back then. In 1960 our favourite was a guy called Chubby Checker.'

'That's someone's name?' said Beth as the two of us fell around laughing.

'Seriously?' I said.

'I've never been more serious in my life,' said Graham. 'Chubby Checker was a huge star back in the day.'

'I guess you and Jeanie listened to his songs on your phones?' I said.

'Very funny,' said Graham. 'Actually, Jeanie's parents had a record player – which was a big deal in 1960. Jeanie saved up and bought Chubby's latest record, 'The Twist'. I didn't feel welcome in Jeanie's house so she'd run inside and put the record on. Then she'd open all the windows, run back outside to the

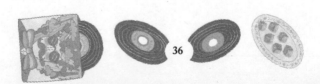

garden, and the two of us would dance as the record played over and over. It was fun until …'

'Until what?' I asked.

'Until Jeanie's parents saw us dancing.'

'Was dancing a crime, back in the day?' asked Beth.

'Well, it wasn't exactly a crime, but some people considered the twist to be a bit indecent – many older people disapproved, and Jeanie's parents – well let's just say they weren't the most progressive people in the world.'

'So what happened then?' I asked.

'One day Jeanie's dad took the record from the record player and snapped it over his knee – and that was the end of 'The Twist' for Jeanie and me. Nowadays, when I see pop videos, I smile at the innocence of how things used to be.'

'So when you couldn't dance any more, how did you spend your time?' asked Beth.

'We did simple things like collecting blackberries and bird-watching. Jeanie was a gifted artist, and she

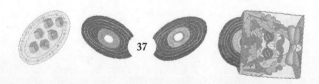

drew pictures of every bird we saw.'

'What else did you do?' I asked, wondering if any-thing was actually fun in the olden days.

'Oh, you know. Reading, swimming in the river, running in the fields, climbing …' Graham had started to smile, but suddenly it was like all the old memories were too much for him. His smile van-ished, and he almost looked ready to cry.

'Jeanie was the best friend I've ever had,' he said.

'She looks nice,' I said. 'How come we've never heard of her before? Do you still hang out with her?'

'Jeanie moved away from here a very long time ago,' he said, 'The last time I saw her was best part of sixty years ago, and now ...'

Then he closed the photo album, and jumped up. 'Don't think it rude of me, girls, but I think this little chat about the olden days is over. Now, who's for a nice cup of blooming tea?'

* * *

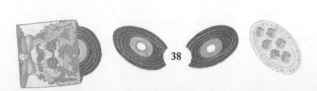

Half an hour later, after two cups of tea and lots of chat about nothing much, Beth and I said goodbye to Graham and headed home. Neither of us said anything while we walked. I had no idea what was going on in Beth's head, but I was dealing with a serious guilt trip.

Then, when we got to our front gate, I put my hand on Beth's arm. 'Hang on a sec', I said. 'Before we go inside, there's something I need to tell you.'

'What?'

'I did something pretty bad back in Graham's house.'

I didn't get why Beth looked relieved, but I kept talking anyway. 'Remember when Graham was in the kitchen making the tea, and you went up to the toilet?' She nodded, and I continued. 'Well – while you were gone I ... I know it was really rude and everything, but I had a look at the letter Graham had left on the living-room table – and you'll never guess

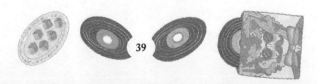

who was mentioned in it?'

'I don't have to guess,' said Beth. 'Because when you went in to the kitchen to ask Graham for a tissue, I looked at the letter too.'

For a second we both laughed – a guilty kind of laugh, like when you do something bad, but then don't feel quite so rotten when you hear that you're not the only one.

'I only did it because ...' we both said the words together.

'I only looked at the letter because I felt sorry for Graham,' I said. 'I wouldn't have touched it otherwise.'

'Same,' she said. 'I was hoping that something in the letter might help us understand why Graham is so sad today.'

'Do you know who Jessica is – the woman who wrote the letter?' I asked.

'Yeah – Dad's talked about her before. She's a distant relation who lives in England now. She's famous

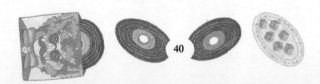

for writing endless boring letters to all her long-lost cousins.'

'You're right about boring,' I said. 'The first page of that letter was the most pathetic thing I've ever read. Who wants to know how many stitches Jessica's nextdoor neighbour got in her leg after she tripped over her cat?'

'I wouldn't mind knowing what happened to the poor cat, though.'

'And the second page of the letter wasn't great either,' I said, laughing. 'Sometimes you can have too much information about someone's tummy bug.'

'Hey, Moll,' said Beth then. 'I'm guessing you saw the PS? I don't suppose you managed to read all of it? I wanted to, but you came back before I had time to turn over the page.'

I closed my eyes and I could still see the words scribbled in at the end of the fifth page. '*Oh, and by the way, Graham, I met someone who had news of that posh girl, Jeanie Cottrell-Herbert. You were friends with*

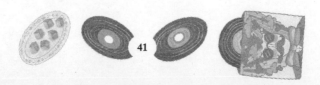

her once upon a time weren't you? Anyway she ...'

I shook my head. 'No,' I said. 'I didn't see the end of the PS either. I was just getting ready to turn over the page when Graham came back into the room.'

'We're not very good spies, are we?' said Beth. 'I wonder what the PS said. I wonder what Jessica was going to say about Jeanie.'

'Maybe Jeanie's coming to live around here again? That'd be so cool. We could try to get Graham and Jeanie together, and it would be totally romantic – like something in one of those soppy movies my mum loves.'

'But Graham seemed so sad today – and he wouldn't be sad if Jeanie was coming back, would he?'

'I guess you're right. It has to be something else.'

'Like what?'

'I know,' I said. 'Maybe Graham had a secret plan to track Jeanie down and ask her out on a date, and Jessica's PS was telling him that she's married to someone else?'

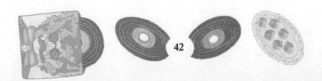

'Poor Graham,' said Beth. 'That'd be awful. Or maybe Jeanie waited for him until recently, and now Jessica was telling him that last year she gave up on him and became a nun.'

'Whatever it is, something in that letter has made Graham sad – and it makes me sad even thinking about it.'

'There's one weird thing though – if Graham and Jeanie were best friends back in the day, how come they haven't seen each other for nearly sixty years? That would *never* happen to you and me. I don't care where you go – I'll always track you down and *make* you be my friend.'

'Same,' I said. 'And since Graham doesn't mind travelling to the ends of the earth to visit people he met for five minutes at a craft fair, how come he never went to see his best friend – no matter what part of the world she ended up in?'

'Maybe boys and girls weren't supposed to be friends back then? Or maybe Jeanie's parents banned

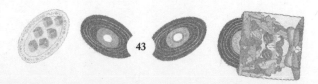

her from seeing Graham because he wasn't posh enough?'

'But you heard him – Jeanie's parents didn't like him, but still they managed to be friends. What could have happened to change that? It doesn't make any sense.'

'Maybe it's got something to do with what my dad said about that time Graham started to act strangely?'

'OMG!' I said, remembering, 'The year Graham and Jeanie danced together was 1960. Something terrible must have happened that summer. But what could it be?'

'It's another mystery,' said Beth. 'A mystery I'd really, really like to solve.'

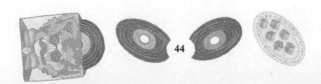

Chapter Five

'You two girls are very interested in the computer tonight,' said Mum. 'Is that part of your homework?'

'We've done all our homework, Charlotte,' said Beth with one of her super-sweet smiles. 'Molly and I are doing some er … historical research.'

'Oh, that's fine,' said Mum, heading back to the kitchen. 'Work away.'

Even though Beth is my very best friend in the whole world, sometimes I feel like thumping her. If I'd made up that stupid excuse about historical research, Mum would have been all over me until she'd figured out the truth. It so isn't fair that Mum's always on *my* case, but she never gives Beth a hard time about anything.

'It *is* history – kind of,' said Beth, almost as if she

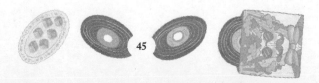

could read my mind. 'Anyway, your mum's gone, so
go ahead and try Instagram.'

I did what she suggested, but once again we couldn't
find any trace of Jeanie Cottrell-Herbert.

'I don't get it,' said Beth. 'Why can't we find her?
It's almost like she never existed.'

'Let's try Facebook,' I said. 'Where all the sad
oldies like our parents hang out.'

But even before I hit the search button, I knew
Jeanie wasn't going to show up.

'This is crazy,' said Beth. 'We've tried every place
we know. If I hadn't seen the photo with my own
eyes, I'd have guessed that Graham made this girl up.'

'Hang on a sec – there's one place we haven't looked
– my mum's favourite site.'

I checked over my shoulder making sure that Mum
hadn't come back into the room. I'm forever laughing
at her for reading the death notices – she'd never let
me forget it if she saw me doing the same.

It didn't take long to find it – the announcement of

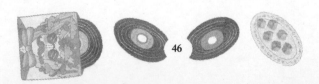

the death of Graham's best friend.

The death has occurred of Jeanie Cottrell-Herbert. Peacefully in Beaumont Hospital, Dublin. Sadly missed by her dear friends, and her devoted dog, Grover. She will always be fondly remembered for her sculptures, which she donated to local parks, for the benefit of the community. No flowers please – if you wish, donate to Animal Welfare, a cause close to Jeanie's heart.

May She Rest in Peace

'Oh!' whispered Beth. 'She's dead. Jeanie is dead. That has to be what Jessica was telling Graham.'

I'd never once met Jeanie. I'd never even heard of her till that day – so I couldn't figure out why I felt so sad. The words seemed so final, almost shouting out at us from the bright white computer screen. I could feel tears coming to my eyes, which was totally weird.

'It doesn't mention any family,' I said. 'No husband or kids or brother or sisters or cousins or anything. How lonely is that?'

'At least she had friends, that's good isn't it?'

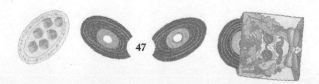

'I guess,' I said. I love Beth, and my other friends, but I couldn't imagine a life without my mum, and dad, and my cousins.

'And she had a dog.'

'Yeah, but – I don't want to sound mean or anything, but if your dog's got to be mentioned in your death notice …'

'Oh, no,' whispered Beth. 'Look at the date.'

'OMG! Jeanie died two months ago.'

'And I guess Graham never knew until he read that letter – he *definitely* doesn't read the death notices.'

'He must have always dreamed that one day the two of them would meet again – and now that's never, ever going to happen.'

'He's lost his chance.'

'Oh, Beth, when I saw how sad he was, I really, really wanted to help him – and now that's impossible. No one can help him with this.'

'But we *have* to do something.'

'Like what?'

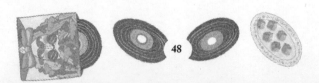

'Let's call over to him tomorrow. Maybe chatting with us will help him to forget about Jeanie – even for a small few minutes.'

'Or maybe he could talk to us *about* her. That could help too.'

I thought back to the time when my dad left. My mum went crazy for a while, and for ages and ages I felt like my life was over – and the only thing that helped was telling Beth how I felt. Sometimes I sat in her house for hours, telling her the same stupid things over and over again – and each time she listened like she'd never heard them before.

'Er, Beth ... I'm sorry if this sounds totally weird, but I don't think I ever told you how good it was to chat to you that time when my dad went away. When I was talking to you, I could kind of believe that life might get to be OK again. So ... er ... thanks.'

She smiled. 'You're welcome – and since we're doing this, did I ever tell you how much it helped to chat about my mum, after you gave me that lovely

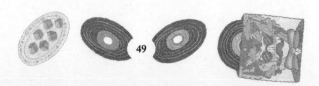

49

birthday letter she wrote for me? Thanks for that too.'

I hugged her. 'It's good to have friends.'

'For sure – so how about we try to be friends to Graham?'

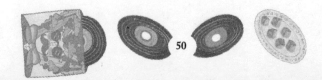

Chapter Six

'Back so soon?' said Graham next day. 'To what do I owe this honour?'

Well, we read your letter, and then we found her online, so we know your best friend died, and we've come to cheer you up.

This *so* wasn't the time for telling the truth.

'Oh, you know,' said Beth. 'Molly and I were just passing, and ...'

'We'd love a cup of tea,' I said, sounding like one of Mum's boring friends. Were we going to go on to say that we'd do anything to get away from the ironing?

Graham didn't seem to mind how lame we sounded. 'Come on in,' he said. 'It's always lovely to see you – so please visit whenever you like – and if I run out of blooming tea, well I'll just have to go visit Chang again, won't I? You go through, and I'll put

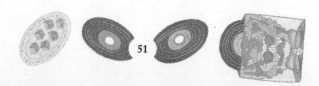

the kettle on.'

'It's gone,' said Beth.

It was the first thing I'd noticed too. Graham's photo album was still on the living room table, but there was no sign of the letter.

'Do you think he knows we read it?' I asked.

'Nah. He thinks we're nice kids.'

'We *are* nice kids. We just …'

'Hey, Moll, what are we going to say about Jeanie?'

'I don't know – it's so awkward, because we're not supposed to know that she's dead.'

'Maybe if we just casually mention her, he'll tell us what happened between them?'

'Good idea. How about you start?'

'Why me?'

'Because he's your uncle?'

'But why does that mean–? Oh, hi, Graham.'

Graham passed the cups around, and then shared out some weird green sweets he'd picked up in a market in Turkey. Then he sat down with a big sigh.

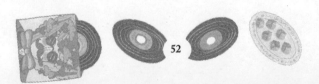

I watched Graham as I sipped my tea and sucked my sweet (that tasted a bit like shampoo). Graham still looked sad.

Being sad made perfect sense, but how was Graham ever going to get over Jeanie if he wouldn't talk about her?

I looked at Beth and tried not to smile, as she slipped a half-sucked sweet out of her mouth and into her pocket. I so wasn't putting a gooey sweet into my pocket, but while Graham was busy stirring his tea, I spat it into a pot plant.

'She died, you know,' said Graham suddenly.

'Who?' I asked, like I had *no* idea who he could possibly be talking about.

'My old friend Jeanie. She died a few months ago – and I never even knew. Once upon a time, the two of us were so very close, and then ...'

He stopped talking. Beth and I looked at each other. I could see she was as embarrassed as I was. I really, really wanted to talk about stupid stuff like

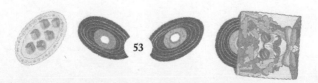

maths homework, and Beth's dad's pathetic jokes – anything except Jeanie, but I knew that wasn't right. It was time to be brave.

'That's so sad,' I said. 'Did you have a fight with her back in the day or something, Graham?'

He looked at me for a minute, and I couldn't make out if he was really angry, or really sad.

'Nothing like that,' he said in the end. 'There was never a single cross word between Jeanie and me.'

'So how come ...?' began Beth.

Graham smiled a sad smile. 'You two aren't going to let this go, are you?'

'Talking's always good,' I said. 'And since Beth and I are here ...'

Graham settled down as much as he could on the lumpy couch. 'It was a very long time ago, and I've never discussed this with anyone, but you're right, maybe it's time to talk about all of this.'

Beth and I looked at each other, then we settled down to listen to Graham's story.

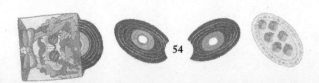

'Jeanie and I first met when I was ten. My father worked in their garden, and at the weekends I helped him out. At first Jeanie stayed away from me – I suspect her parents had told her to. But little by little we got to know each other. Then one day, Jeanie came to me in tears, telling me about a kitten who was stuck on the garage roof. She wanted to climb up and rescue it, but her mother nearly had a conniption at the very thought of that. Instead, I climbed up and rescued the kitten.'

'That's so sweet,' I said.

'Well, the kitten wasn't very sweet,' said Graham. 'It was a dirty, spitting ball of fury, with sharp claws and weeping eyes. Most girls I knew would have run a mile, but Jeanie cradled it like it was the most perfect thing she'd ever seen. As we brought the kitten back to its mother I could see that Jeanie was a very special girl – she was both gentle and brave – and all

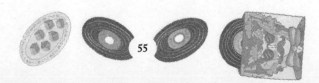

I wanted in the world was to be her friend.'

'Awww!' said Beth. 'So cute.'

'Anyway,' continued Graham. 'Jeanie went to boarding school, so I only saw her in the holidays. She'd write to tell me when she was coming home, and when she got here, I'd be waiting.'

'Where's here?' asked Beth. 'Did you live around here back then?'

'I lived over on The Green,' said Graham, 'and Jeanie lived in Orchard House.'

'Where the fancy hotel is?' I asked.

'That's the place,' said Graham. 'That's where she grew up – but her family moved from there many years ago now.'

'That's so cool,' I said. 'You must have had heaps of fun playing there.'

'Well, it wasn't quite like that,' said Graham. 'I only went inside once, and Jeanie's parents made me feel so unwelcome, I had no desire to repeat the experi-ence – well, to be honest, I was too scared to go back

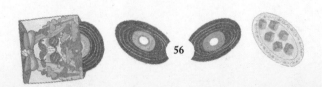

56

inside – Jeanie's parents seemed terrifying to me.'

'That must have been a problem for you and Jeanie?' said Beth.

'Not as much as you might think. We didn't spend any time at my house either – Jeanie and I preferred to be outside.'

This was sounding like a happy-ever-after story – except Beth and I knew for sure there wasn't going to be a happy ending.

'I was just thirteen that last summer we spent together – the summer of 1960,' said Graham. 'Jeanie's thirteenth birthday was in July, and her parents forced her to have a party with her posh boarding school friends. I wasn't invited, but Jeanie saved me a huge slice of cake, and afterwards she told me about the hideous frilly dresses her friends wore, and how upset one girl got when she spilt a few cake-crumbs on her skirt. Jeanie was an excellent mimic, and the two of us laughed for a long time at her impersonation of another girl who was

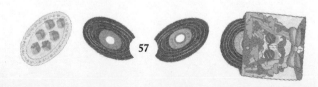

afraid of spiders.'

'Jeanie sounds funny,' I said.

'She was,' said Graham. 'She was so ... alive. She was a little younger than me, but she was tall and tough. She could run as fast as me, and she was far better at swimming. Her parents probably thought I would lead her into mischief, but in fact the opposite was true. Jeanie was the one who was always daring me to run faster, climb higher. But then ...'

He stopped talking and I was afraid he wouldn't say any more.

'But then,' he continued. 'As the weeks passed that summer, and as July turned to August, things changed. Jeanie began to act strangely.'

'Like how?' asked Beth.

'It's hard to explain. At the time I couldn't figure it out.'

'So give us an example of stuff she did,' I suggested.

'At first Jeanie stopped doing her drawings,' said Graham. 'She finished one of me that she'd been

working on, and then she wouldn't do any more. She said drawing was stupid and that she'd never had any real talent anyway.'

'But you said—', began Beth.

'She had a very special talent,' said Graham. 'There was no doubt about it.'

'I'd love to see that drawing of you,' I said. 'Have you still got it?'

'I very much wish I had,' he said. 'Jeanie promised to give it to me as a parting gift when she went back to school, but ... well that never happened.'

'What else was strange, that summer?' asked Beth.

'It's difficult to explain,' said Graham. 'It was as if Jeanie was losing her nerve. She became cautious, and timid – like her adventurous spirit was starting to evaporate. One day she threw her bike into the shed and said that cycling was boring.'

'Maybe she was just growing up?' I suggested. 'It happens, you know.'

'Indeed,' said Graham. 'I can see it before my very

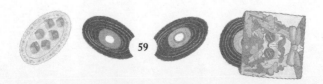

eyes with you two – but where Jeanie was concerned, there was something else going on – the change happened too quickly, and was too pronounced.'

'Any idea *why* she changed?' I asked.

'Not really,' he said. 'I teased her about it. I said she was getting too like her posh friends, but she denied it. She said she'd never end up like them.'

'Did you believe her?' asked Beth.

'I wanted to,' he said. 'But I wasn't so sure. I felt she was becoming a different person. I thought I was losing her, and I didn't know what to do about it. I simply wanted to things to stay the same forever. Maybe that's why—'

And then, just when it looked like we were getting somewhere, my phone rang.

'Have you forgotten we're going to town to buy new hockey jackets for you and Beth?' said Mum. 'We need to leave in ten minutes.'

She was right. Graham's story was so interesting, I'd totally forgotten about town and hockey and

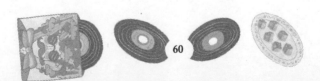

everything else.

'Mum sounds mad,' I said. 'We've got to go. Sorry, Graham, but ...'

'That's OK,' he said. 'I've kept this story to myself for fifty-something years. Another few days won't hurt.'

'But we can come back and talk about it some more right?' asked Beth.

'Please?' I said. 'Otherwise it would be like reading a book and finding that the last few pages were missing.'

'Or like when Dad turns off the TV in the middle of the best movie ever,' said Beth.

'Come back anytime you wish,' said Graham. 'And we can continue our little chat. And don't worry, next time I won't force feed you with Turkish sweets. They don't seem to agree with young girls, though no doubt the sugar will give my pot plant a little lift.'

'OMG,' I said totally embarrassed. 'I'm so sorry.

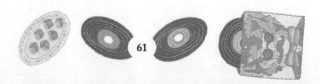

It was …'

'Don't worry about it at all,' he said. 'Now run along, and I'll see you when I see you.'

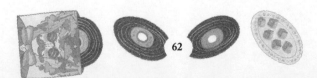

Chapter Seven

'You were telling us about how Jeanie was changing that summer when you were thirteen,' I said.

It was a few days later, and Beth and I were back in Graham's place.

'Ah,' said Graham. 'So I was.'

'And?' I was trying not to sound impatient.

Graham gave a big sigh. 'I'm trying to tell the truth about what happened, but I fear you two girls will think less of me when you hear it.'

'That's *never* going to happen,' said Beth. 'All this happened like a thousand years ago – and you were still a kid.'

'And we know you'd never do anything mean,' I added.

'That's very sweet of you,' said Graham. 'Wait and hear my story though, before you decide. When I'm

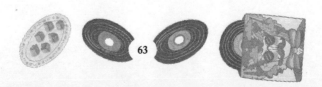

finished, maybe you'll think differently of me.'

'No way!' said Beth. 'But if you don't get on with the story, we might go ahead and die of boredom or something.'

'OK, OK,' he said. 'If you're all sitting comfortably, I'll begin. As I said, Jeanie had been acting strangely, and I was afraid of losing her. It was a lovely sunny day, one of the best we'd had that year. It was already halfway through August, and I had a horrible feeling that things were coming to an end.'

'How do you mean?' asked Beth.

'It's hard to explain,' said Graham. 'I was old enough to understand how seasons come and go, but I couldn't shake the thought that Jeanie and I would never again share such a perfect summer. It was ...'

He closed his eyes, and for a minute it seemed that he wasn't going to say any more – and there was *no* way I was going to let that happen.

'So what happened that day in August?' I asked.

Graham opened his eyes. 'Jeanie was listless and

just wanted to lie in the sun,' he said. 'But I per-
suaded her to come to our special spot in the woods.
We collected blackberries, but even though Jeanie
usually competed with me, rushing to fill her basket
first, that day she gave up when she'd barely picked a
handful of fruit. It seems stupid now, but at the time
I was irritated and cross.'

I couldn't help feeling sorry for the young Graham,
confused and afraid of losing his best friend.

'So what happened next?' I asked.

Graham didn't say anything for a long time. When
he did speak, it was in a flat, dead kind of voice, like
he'd been practising what to say.

'I suggested that we climb our favourite tree –
something Jeanie had always liked doing. She didn't
want to at first, but I ... encouraged her. I said she was
turning into a coward like her posh friends, and that
soon she'd be afraid of her own shadow.'

'I'm guessing she wasn't happy about that,' said
Beth.

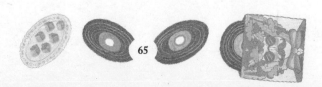

'At first she pouted a bit – and then, a second later, it was like a miracle. She tossed her hair and laughed, and in that instant it was as if the old Jeanie had come back to me.

'I'm not afraid,' she said. 'I'm not afraid of *any-thing*. I'll go first and I'll climb higher than we've ever climbed before. You wait here and watch me.'

'So Jeanie climbed the tree?' said Beth.

'Yes,' said Graham. 'She climbed the tree – like she had a hundred times before – when she was almost at the top she clung to the last substantial branch and shouted down to me. "It's glorious up here,' she said. 'I feel as if I'm flying. Come join me – there's room for both of us."'

'And?' I said.

'And in that moment everything in my world was good again,' said Graham. 'It was as if the sun had been hiding behind a cloud, and now it had re-emerged and was bathing me in its beautiful warmth. Jeanie was happy and wild and brave. She wanted me to be

with her, and there was a whole future of adventure and friendship waiting for us.'

It all sounded wonderful – except for the fact that Beth and I already knew that things weren't going to turn out the way Graham hoped.

'So I started to climb,' said Graham. 'I couldn't wait to get close to her … and I was concentrating on finding good foot and hand-holds, so … so I didn't even see what happened. Maybe a branch broke, or maybe she lost her grip – all I knew was that Jeanie made a small, surprised cry, and then she was tumbling past me. I leaned out and grabbed her, but the momentum was too much and her hand slipped from mine – and she continued to fall, and fall and fall, until she hit the ground with a soft thud.'

'That's so scary,' said Beth.

'I went into a complete panic,' said Graham. 'I scrambled down from the tree, and ran to where she was lying. She was still and pale, almost as if she were asleep. I touched her arm, but she didn't move. I ran to

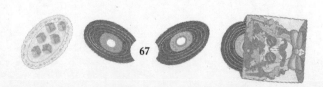

the nearest house and they called an ambulance. I ran back to Jeanie, and stroked her hair and whispered to her. It felt like a lifetime, but it was probably only minutes before the ambulance showed up. Someone had called Jeanie's parents, but the ambulance arrived before they got there.'

'And did Jeanie wake up?' I asked.

He shook his head. 'I watched as they put the stretcher into the ambulance, but she remained perfectly still. I wanted to travel with her, but the ambulance men wouldn't let me. They told me to "run away home". So that's what I did – and ... I never saw my lovely friend again.'

'And what did your parents say when you got home?' I asked.

'Well, here's the thing,' said Graham. 'I never told my parents what happened.'

'You never ...?' said Beth. 'But ...'

'You have no idea how bad I felt that day. Jeanie was my best friend, and she had fallen because of me.

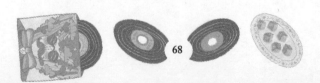

If I hadn't teased her about being a coward, she never would have climbed the tree. She never would have ...' Graham put his head in his hands. 'The whole thing was all my fault. I was so ashamed.'

'But that's crazy, Graham,' said Beth. 'You can't blame yourself! Kids tease each other all the time.'

'It's what kids do,' I agreed. 'How could you have known that Jeanie was going to fall? How could you—?'

Now Graham looked up at us, and his huge, sad brown eyes made me want to cry. 'I was older than her,' he said softly. 'I should have known better. I should have looked out for her – but I didn't. Now if you two girls don't mind, I think I need to be on my own now.'

Beth and I so didn't want to leave him, but he ignored all of our arguments.

'I've never told that story to a single soul,' he said. 'And maybe talking helps in the long run, but I confess that right now I don't feel entirely wonderful, so

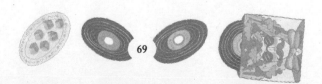

if you'll excuse me, I'm going to lie down for a while.'

'Can we call again tomorrow?' asked Beth as he walked us to the door.

'Well, I'm not really.....'

'If you don't promise that we can visit tomorrow, then we're not leaving you,' I said. I don't usually talk to adults like that, but Graham wasn't like all the other adults – which might be why Beth and I loved him so much.

'OK, I give in,' said Graham, giving the tiniest flicker of a smile. 'You can visit me tomorrow – and in the meantime, don't worry about me – I'm going to tuck myself up in bed with a good book – a cure for most problems.'

So we both hugged him, and then he closed the door behind us.

* * *

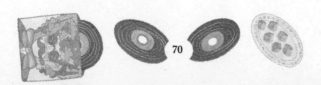

Beth spoke first. 'That's the saddest thing I've ever heard,' she said. 'Imagine the poor boy, feeling guilty for all those years?'

'I know,' I said. 'It's terrible, but we have to find out what happened next. We know Jeanie didn't die that day – because that only happened this year. She lived for years and years after the accident. She did sculptures good enough to be displayed in parks. She got to have friends and a dog and everything. So how come Graham never saw her again?'

'That's still the mystery,' said Beth. 'And I totally hate mysteries.'

'We *have* to hear the rest of the story,' I said. 'We just have to.'

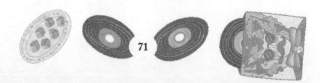

Chapter Eight

'You two don't give up easily,' said Graham the next day. 'I think you might have been terriers in your last life.'

'Thanks a lot,' I said. 'I always dreamed of being compared to a small, hairy creature with pointy teeth.'

'Anyway,' said Beth. 'Enough with the small talk. You know we want to hear the rest of the story, Graham.'

'We're not being nosy,' I added. (Which was only half true.) 'But it's not healthy having all this bad stuff locked up in your head. If you don't talk about it, you'll never get over it.'

'But ...' began Graham.

'Trust us,' I said. 'You were telling us how poor Jeanie had just gone off in the ambulance, and you were being all tough and brave.'

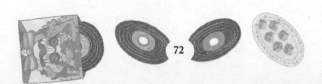

'I didn't feel very brave,' said Graham. 'I felt scared and sad and alone.'

'You're not alone now,' said Beth, patting his hand.

'So I didn't sleep a wink that night,' he said. 'And next morning I was too afraid to call over to Orchard House, so I went to the phone box on the main street, and telephoned. The housekeeper answered and told me that Jeanie's parents were at the hospital with her. When she told me that Jeanie was awake, and talking, I thought I was going to die from happiness. Then I asked if it would be alright to visit Jeanie in the hospital, and the housekeeper went quiet. In the end she said she thought that was a very bad idea, and that I should stay away from the family for a while.'

'So you just gave up?' said Beth. 'That doesn't sound like you.'

He smiled. 'No, it's not like me – and that's not what I did. I went home and wrote a very long letter to Jeanie, and posted it to the hospital.'

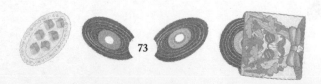

'And did she reply?' I asked, afraid I already knew the answer to my question.

'No,' said Graham. 'Days and days passed, but she didn't reply. So I wrote again, and then I wrote to her home, but still nothing. I had no idea where she was – or how she was.'

'That's awful,' I said.

'It was indeed awful,' said Graham. 'I telephoned her house a number of times, but as soon as the housekeeper heard my voice, she hung up.'

'But this isn't a huge big city,' said Beth. 'Everyone knows everyone else around here. Surely someone could have told you what was going on?'

He shook his head. 'Jeanie's family lived here, but they were never part of the community. Mostly they kept themselves hidden behind the high walls of their house. They didn't shop here or socialise here. My dad had stopped working for them by then, so no one really knew them at all, except for me.'

'So what happened next?' asked Beth.

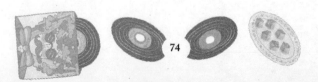

'It was nearly time for Jeanie to go back to board-ing school, and if that happened, I knew there would be no opportunity to see her again until Christmas. I simply couldn't let that happen. I missed her so much, it was like a physical pain, and ...'

'And what?' I asked, dying for him to continue.

'And I knew I had to be brave,' said Graham. 'I knew I had to go to Orchard House.'

'And when you got there?' prompted Beth.

'I think it's time for tea,' said Graham.

* * *

Fifteen minutes later we were sipping yet another cup of blooming tea – this time flavoured with vanilla and lemon, like the nicest ice-cream you could ever dream of.

'So I went up the drive,' said Graham. 'And the sound of my bicycle wheels seemed terribly loud on the thick gravel.'

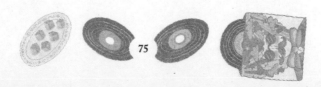

Graham didn't even need us to prompt him – it was like he couldn't stop talking, now that he'd finally got going.

'I didn't dare go to the front door, so I went around the back where the delivery boys usually called. I knocked on the door and the sound echoed through the house, announcing my arrival. I hoped the housekeeper would answer, but then I heard high heels coming towards the front door, and I knew it had to be Jeanie's mother – Jeanie had told me that she dressed every day as if she were going out to a fancy party, even if she didn't plan to set a foot out-side the house. Part of me wanted to race down the drive and never come back, and only the thought of seeing Jeanie made me stay there. So Jeanie's mother opened the door and ...'

'And what?' I asked.

Graham looked scared, like he was thirteen again, and standing outside Orchard House. For a second, I could almost see the young boy he used to be. He

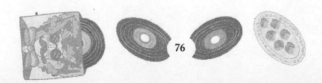

took a deep breath, and continued.

'And Jeanie's mother looked at me as if I were a piece of dirt that the cat had dragged in. "You!" she said. "How dare you show your face around here? Jeanie could have been killed in that fall – and it's all your fault." And now the urge to run was almost overwhelming, but still I stayed.'

'That was brave of you,' said Beth.

Graham half-smiled. 'Brave or stupid, I'm not sure which. Anyway, I found my voice, and asked if I could see Jeanie. And her mother gave me a cruel, cold look. "You won't be seeing her again," she said. "Jeanie leaves hospital in the morning – and she will be going straight to school." But I knew that couldn't be right. Jeanie's school wasn't due to open until the following week – I knew the date – it had been imprinted in my mind since the beginning of the summer.'

'So Jeanie's mother lied to you?' I said. 'That wasn't very nice.'

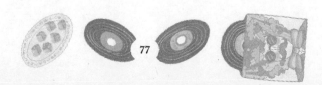

He shook his head, sadly. 'She wasn't nice, but she wasn't lying either.'

'I don't get it,' said Beth.

'I didn't get it either,' said Graham. 'So I asked her why the date had changed – and then Jeanie's mother started to cry. And I was so embarrassed, I didn't know where to look, or what to say. And then she started to shout at me and even though it was so many years ago, I can still recall her exact words. "Jeanie will not be returning to her old school," she said. "Everything is different now. She will be attending a special school. Don't you understand, you stupid boy? Jeanie is blind. She is going to spend the rest of her life in an institution. Now go away, or I will have my husband call the police."'

'OMG!' I said. 'Jeanie went blind. The poor girl – and poor you. It must have been an awful shock to hear that about your lovely friend.'

Graham nodded. 'My lovely friend lost her sight because of me.'

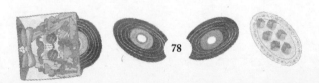

'It was an accident,' I said. 'It so wasn't your fault.'

'You can't blame yourself,' said Beth. 'And anyway, Jeanie's mother was crazy. I get that she was upset and everything, but why did she say Jeanie couldn't have friends? Why did she say she had to live in a home for the rest of her life? A girl I used to know had a visually-impaired brother, and he had an amazing life. He goes skiing and jogging and last I heard he was planning to climb Mount Everest.'

'That's the way things should be, ' said Graham. 'But it was very different back then. Any kind of a disability was almost an embarrassment – and all kinds of wonderful people who were deemed "not quite perfect" were banished from the rest of society.'

'That's so sad,' I said. 'And that was the end of you and Jeanie?'

'Pretty much,' said Graham. 'I sent many, many letters to Jeanie over the next few months. I knew she couldn't read them, but I hoped someone would read them to her.'

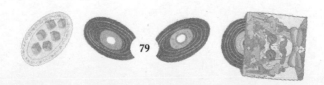

'Well, her evil mother wasn't going to do it, that's for sure,' I said. 'But did anyone else help you? Did you ever get a reply to your letters?'

'Not a single word. And at Christmas, when I knew she'd be home for holidays, I braved Orchard House again, but this time I met Jeanie's dad. He told me that Jeanie wanted nothing to do with me, that she was ashamed of ever spending time with me – and then he chased me away with one of Jeanie's old hockey sticks.'

'He sounds like the wicked monster from a fairy-tale,' I said.

Except fairytales are supposed to have happy endings.

'Did you believe what he said about Jeanie being ashamed of your friendship?' asked Beth.

'I did at the time,' said Graham. 'You young girls are sophisticated and worldly wise, but I was a very innocent young man. I didn't think to question what he said.'

'And now?' I asked.

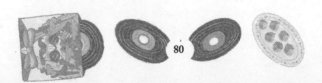

'Well now I'm not so sure any more – and I never had the chance to find out. A few months later Orchard House was sold and the family moved away. There was no Google or Facebook back then, and I had no way of finding out where they went.'

'I'm so sorry, Graham,' said Beth.

'I've thought about Jeanie a lot in recent years,' said Graham. 'I thought about trying to find her – but the guilt and the shame always held me back ... but still – I always hoped that fate would bring us together – I always hoped that one day Jeanie and I would meet again – but ... well that's not going to happen now is it? That ship has sailed without me.'

Beth hugged him. 'Oh, Graham,' she said. 'You poor thing. I wish we could do something to help.'

He gave a small, sad smile. 'You listened,' he said.

* * *

'That's the saddest story I've ever heard,' I said as

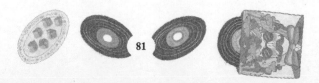

Beth and I walked home. 'I wish there was something we could do to help Graham.'

'There *is* one thing ...'

'What's that?'

'We could ... you know ... go to Rico's and go back to when Graham and Jeanie were friends and ...'

I stopped walking. 'You think time-travelling's the answer to everything, Beth! We can't make it so that Graham doesn't suggest climbing the tree. We can't stop Jeanie from falling. We can't change—'

'Face it, Molly. We have *no* idea what we can and can't do when we go back to the past. I know I couldn't save my mum ...'

'And I'm so sorry about that,' I said hugging her.

She hugged me back and then pulled away. 'But we can't just do nothing. You saw how sad and guilty Graham feels. We're his friends and we *have* to try and help him.'

I didn't argue – mostly because I knew she was right.

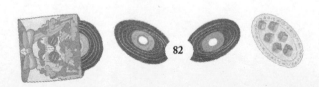

'So we've got a plan?'

She grinned. 'Sure we've got a plan. It might be a plan that's doomed to fail, but I guess that's got to be better than no plan at all.'

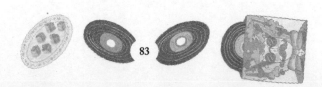

Chapter Nine

*a*fter school the next day, Beth pushed open the door of Rico's shop, and I followed her inside. Once again, Rico was standing there polishing one of his many tiny glass bottles. I wondered if glass wears away if you polish it for long enough. Rico looked up and didn't seem surprised to see us; that guy seriously freaks me out. Only the thought of Graham's sad face kept me from racing back outside to the real world.

'Er ... hi,' said Beth. 'Do you mind if my friend and I ...?'

Rico put down his polishing cloth and smiled the kind of smile that doesn't make you feel any better than you did before.

'You know the way,' he said. 'See you soon!'

Beth and I slipped past him, and through the black curtain. Just like the last time, it was warm and dark

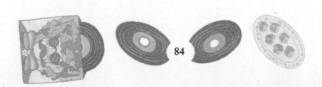

and creepy.

'Concentrate on where we need to be, Molly,' whispered Beth. 'Keep thinking about Graham and Winnie and how we can help them.'

I tried to do what she said, but the weird cinnamon smell kept distracting me. I held tightly to Beth's hand and then we tumbled forwards.

'OMG,' said Beth as she opened her eyes. 'Good old Rico.'

I grabbed Beth's arm and pulled her off the road, as a weird, noisy car beeped at us.

'Either Rico's worked his magic or everyone around here's heading for an antique car show,' I said.

Beth giggled, and I was glad that her sense of humour is good at time-travelling – I love lots of things about my best friend, including the fact that she laughs at my jokes even when they're pretty lame.

'Let's not waste time,' said Beth. 'We need to find out if we're when we need to be.'

'Agreed,' I said. 'Let's ask that woman who looks

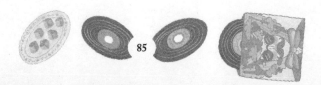

like she's wearing a lampshade on her head instead of a hat!'

We crossed the road again, and went up to the woman.

'Er, hi,' said Beth. 'Do you mind if we ask you a question?'

'Of course not,' said the woman, smiling. 'How can I help you? Are you lost?'

We probably *were* lost, but that wasn't our biggest problem.

'Could you tell us what year it is, please?' I asked.

'It's 1960,' said the woman. 'Oh, but you must know that already.'

'We didn't, honestly,' said Beth. 'We get confused about stuff like that. And could you tell us please what month it is?'

'It's August,' said the woman. Then her smile faded. 'You're being cheeky, aren't you?'

'No,' I said. 'We're not being cheeky at all. You see Beth and I ...' I stopped talking – how could I possibly begin to explain?

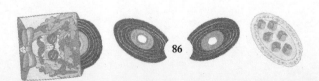

'Children these days!' said the woman. 'You simply don't know how to respect adults.'

'That's what my mum always says too,' I began. 'She ...', but now the woman looked really cross, so I just smiled and thanked her and she walked away muttering bad stuff about us.

'August 1960,' said Beth. 'That's so cool. Graham said that's when Jeanie's accident happened, remember? Rico might be seriously creepy, but it looks like he's got it right again.'

'But we don't know the exact date,' I said. 'And I so don't fancy asking that cross woman any more questions.'

'You're right,' sighed Beth. 'And even if we find out today's exact date, it won't help us. All we know is that the accident happened around the middle of August. We should have asked Graham for more details.'

'But we didn't – and for all we know, Jeanie might have fallen out of the tree two weeks ago, or last week, or maybe even five minutes ago while we were

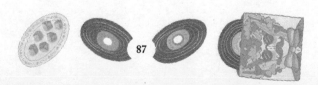

talking to that woman.'

'So what are we waiting for? Let's go find Graham and Jeanie.'

* * *

In the present, Beth and I could easily find the way to Orchard House, but in the past, everything is just different enough to make getting around totally confusing. Nothing seemed to be in the right place any more.

'How did people survive without Google maps?' sighed Beth as we got lost for the tenth time. 'Everyone from the olden days should get special medals, just for managing to get to school and back. I'm guessing some people set out for school and were never seen again.'

'Oh, here's a woman,' I said, giggling. 'Let's ask her.'

'Er, excuse me,' I said. 'Do you know the way to Orchard Road?'

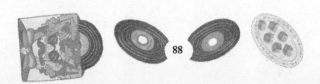

'Of course I do,' said the woman. 'It's very easy. You go to the end of this road, take a left at the bridge, then you take the second right, go left at the crossroads, left again, then right at the old water pump and then it's the next right.'

'Did you get any of that?' I asked when the woman was gone.

'I got the first bit,' said Beth. 'And after that I couldn't keep track any more.'

'And since when was there a water pump anywhere around here?'

'I guess we should go as far as the bridge, and ask again?'

But before we even got to the bridge, Beth stopped suddenly.

'OMG!' she said. 'At last I know where we are. Look – there's our school.'

'You're right,' I said. 'I think.'

It had to be our school, but ... it looked too new and shiny and strange. It was smaller than it's sup-

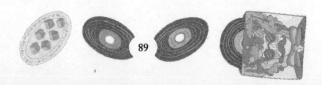

posed to be. The car park was a hockey pitch, and the science lab was a bed of red and yellow roses.

'This is so cool,' said Beth. 'I'd love to see what our school was like in the olden days. Let's peep in a window.'

I really wanted to get going to Orchard House, but Beth was right – it would be cool to see what our school looked like long before we got there.

'I guess,' I said. 'But it's August, remember? School will be closed so there won't be much to see.'

'Exactly!' said Beth. 'One quick look in the window and then we can get pack to our mission.'

I followed her through the gates and along the driveway, (which was gravel instead of tarmac.)

We peeped through the first window we came to. In the classroom, a teacher in a long black cloak was writing on a blackboard, and lines of girls were copying her words into notebooks.

'OMG!' said Beth as the two of us ducked down behind a bush. 'School's open. I don't get it.'

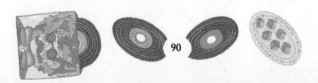

'Hang on a sec,' I said, picking a thorn from my finger. 'Remember when those kids wrote the history of the school last year? Didn't they say that it was a private school, back in the day? And that only girls came here? And that it was different to all the other schools around here?'

'Yeah, I remember that.'

'So maybe they had different holidays?'

'Yikes! Poor them. Imagine having to go to school in August?'

'Anyway, if school's open, I think we need to get out of here, fast. I think we need—'

'Goodness gracious me! I cannot believe my eyes. Get up from there and act like young ladies.'

Beth and I turned around to see a familiar, very cross-looking woman staring at us.

'Miss Gallagher?' I said as Beth and I stood up and dusted bits of grass off our clothes.

I shut my eyes for a second, trying to do the sums in my head. Could my maths teacher (the scariest

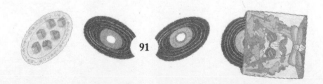

teacher in the world) have been a teacher in 1960? Wouldn't that make her something like a hundred and fifty years old?

'*Mrs* Gallagher,' said the woman, and then I remembered our maths teacher boasting that her mum had been a teacher in our school too. This was getting very weird very fast. Did our maths teacher learn all her scary tricks from her mother?

'Stand up straight and look at me while I'm speaking to you,' said Mrs Gallagher.

I could feel my hands starting to shake. Beth squeezed my arm. It was nice of her, but her hand was shaking too, so I didn't feel a whole lot better.

'What are your names?' asked Mrs Gallagher, pointing her bony finger at us.

'Er ... I'm Molly,' I said. 'And this is Beth.'

'First years,' I presume,' said Mrs Gallagher. 'I haven't had time to get to know you all yet – but mark my words – I'll remember you two – I've never seen such a display – rolling in the earth like cornerboys.'

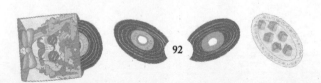

I had no clue what a cornerboy was, and Beth and I hadn't been rolling around on the earth anyway, but it didn't look like Mrs Gallagher was up for a reasonable debate.

'Er ... we're sorry,' said Beth.

'And what on earth has happened to your uniforms?'

Nothing had happened to our uniforms. I was wearing my skirt and my jumper with the proper crest. My shirt was buttoned up properly, and my tie was tied. Even mean old Mr Heaslip, the head of the uniform police in our school would have been happy.

But then I looked in the window again and saw that, like us, the girls inside were wearing green uniforms – but theirs were totally weird and old-fashioned.

'Er ... we ...' I began, before I realised that we weren't actually supposed to answer the question.

'WHERE ARE YOUR GYMSLIPS?' Now Mrs Gallagher's face was going red. She didn't look like

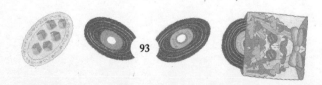

she'd want to hear the story about Rico and Graham and Jeanie. She didn't look like she'd listen to our explanation that we weren't supposed to be in first year for nearly sixty years.

'Er ... we didn't know gym class was on now,' said Beth. 'We ...'

'Your insolence is astounding,' said Mrs Gallagher, grabbing Beth and me by our arms. 'You can report for detention later, but now it's time for your Latin class – and if you haven't learned your verbs you will be in very hot water indeed.'

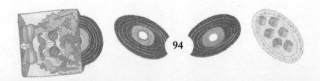

Chapter Ten

Mrs Gallagher dragged us in the front door, and through the big space where the library is supposed to be. My arm was hurting and I wondered if that kind of stuff was supposed to be OK in 1960.

Finally Mrs Gallagher let go of our arms to open a classroom door, and then she practically pushed us inside.

When the girls saw the teacher they all stood up – 'Good morning, Mrs Gallagher,' they said in a chorus. They were all wearing ugly uniforms and staring at Beth and me like we were aliens.

'Go and find a desk – near the front – where I can keep an eye on you,' said Mrs Gallagher, pushing us away from her.

I rubbed my arm wondering if I'd be taking the print of her fingers back to the present with me. Then

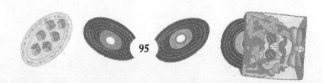

I followed Beth to an empty desk in the second row. I thought about sitting down, but changed my mind when I noticed that everyone else was still standing up.

Everyone said a prayer together, and then Mrs Gallagher said, 'You may sit.'

For the first time I looked properly at the desk Beth and I had chosen. It was huge and heavy, like something out of a museum. The seat was joined onto the desk, and looked really narrow. Was this some kind of 1960s torture? Was it designed so there was no way you could fall asleep in class? Did girls in 1960 have smaller bums than us?

Beth and I were just trying to balance ourselves on the narrow seat when I heard the girl next to us laughing.

'You two are hilarious,' she said.

She didn't sound mean, but I don't like being laughed at when I have no idea what I've done wrong. Then I heard a series of loud bangs and I noticed that everyone else was flipping their narrow seats down,

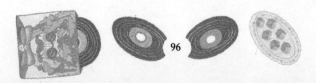

so even though they still looked hard and uncom-
fortable, they were at least wide enough to sit on
properly. Beth and I copied everyone else and I tried
not to feel totally stupid as we sat down.

'Who knew 1960s desks could be so complicated?'
said Beth, making me feel a small bit better. 'They
should come with an instruction manual.'

Mrs Gallagher was at the top of the room, taking a
big stack of books out of a cupboard.

'Hey,' whispered the girl who'd been laughing at us.
'I've never seen you two before. Where on earth did
you come from?'

'Er ... we're new,' said Beth. 'Today's our first day.'

Then I remembered what Mrs Gallagher had said
about gymslips. I didn't figure that 1960 gym would
be a whole lot of fun, but Latin sounded totally scary.
And I so didn't like what Mrs Gallagher had said
about verbs and hot water.

'Aren't we supposed to be at gym class now?' I said.

'Gym class?' said the girl. 'What's that? And why

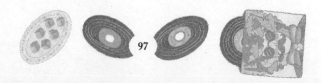

do you think we should be there?'

'Because the teacher said we should be wearing gymslips.'

The girl laughed in my face, which was a bit rude.

'What's so funny?' I asked.

The girl pointed at her ugly uniform with its belt and fat pleats. 'This is a gymslip,' she said. 'And we wear it to every lesson – except not to gym, because I haven't got the foggiest idea what that is. What kind of uniforms are you two wearing?'

'Why didn't we plan this better?' I whispered to Beth. 'We should have known that our regular school uniforms would make us stand out too much in the past.'

'Oh, yeah,' whispered Beth back, giggling. 'We definitely should have worn those 1960s uniforms we keep at the back of our wardrobes for times like these.'

The girl was staring at us like we were aliens. 'Where did you say you came from again?' she asked.

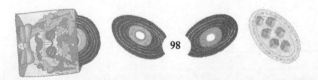

98

We come from a place about two kilometres and fifty years away.

'Er ... we come from ...', began Beth, but before she could finish, Mrs Gallagher banged on her desk.

'Silence!' she shouted, and immediately everyone stopped talking. 'Take out your homework,' she said, 'and you shall take turns to call out the answers.'

All the girls started to dig around in their weird old-fashioned schoolbags.

I tapped the girl next to me. 'We haven't got any homework. What are we supposed to do?'

The girl smiled at us. 'Don't worry about it,' she whispered. 'Now that Mrs Gallagher's sitting down, she won't move any more. Here, you can have my English and Domestic Science homework. Just open any old page – Mrs G won't check.'

'Thanks,' I said. 'By the way, I'm Molly, and this is Beth.'

The girl leaned over and shook our hands, like we were making a deal or something. 'I'm Rita,' she said.

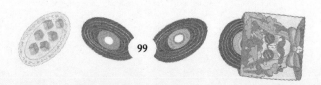

'Rita Walshe.'

'OMG!' said Beth. 'You're ...'

Suddenly I could see past the girl's pigtails and her shapeless school uniform. I managed to see the same girl – except much older and prettier, wearing really cool clothes and with her hair tied up in a fancy bun.

'OMG!' I said too. 'I don't believe it. You're Rita Walshe – the famous opera singer. My granny loves your records. She even went to see you once in ...'

'What on *earth* are you talking about?' said Rita, going red. 'I like to sing, but I'd never in my wildest dreams imagine that ... I don't like singing in public ... I'm too shy to even join the school choir. I never ... I simply couldn't ...'

I so badly wanted to tell her the wonderful future that was waiting for her – but how could I? How could I even begin to explain what I knew and how I knew it? So I just smiled at our new friend.

'You should believe in yourself,' I said. 'And one day I'm sure you'll go on to wonderful things. One

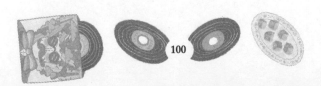

day you might even ...'

Suddenly Mrs Gallagher slammed a book on the table and everyone stopped whispering. 'Homework time,' she said. 'Question one – why don't you start, Molly?'

I jumped. Mrs Gallagher was staring at me like she *knew* I was going to fail. She was half-smiling like she was dying to give me a totally cruel 1960s punishment. I looked down at the open exercise book in front of me. There was lots of beautiful handwriting in it, but it looked like a recipe. I didn't know much about Latin, but I guessed the ingredient list for the gross-sounding Russian Fish Pie wasn't going to help me a whole lot.

Then Rita poked me in the arm. 'Amo – amas – amat,' she whispered.

It sounded like a Hogwarts spell, but what did I know?

'Er ... a mo ... a mas ... a mat,' I said.

'That's right,' said Mrs Gallagher, looking disap-

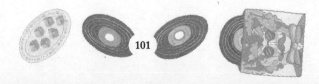

pointed. 'But be a bit quicker next time. Now Beth, can you share your answer to question two with us?'

'O farmer, you see the church,' whispered Rita.

She had to be kidding, but Beth said the words and Mrs Gallagher nodded. 'Question three, Eleanor,' she said. 'And get a move on. We'd like to have this homework corrected before 1961.'

* * *

The next forty minutes were the most boring of my whole entire life. School *so* wasn't fun back in 1960. As soon as all the homework was corrected, the teacher called out lists of words, and the girls repeated them after her, like well-trained parrots. Next, Mrs Gallagher wrote loads of stuff on the blackboard, and the girls spent twenty minutes copying it into their notebooks.

'This is such a waste of time,' whispered Beth as the two of us pretended to write into Rita's exercise

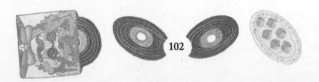

books. 'Couldn't the teacher just photocopy all this stuff and give it to us?'

'Or give us a link so we could look it up online?' I suggested. 'We've only been here for an hour, but I miss the present so much.'

A few minutes later, a bell rang. Everyone closed their books and we all stood up and said another prayer.

When Mrs Gallagher left the room, Rita turned to Beth and me.

'It's lunchtime now,' she said. 'And afterwards we've got music appreciation and history. We can sit together if you like – and I can help you with the things you don't know.'

She was being really nice, but Rita had no clue that for Beth and me, that very minute was ancient history – and that none of the music we appreciated had been written yet.

'Lunch with Rita sounds fun,' said Beth. 'What do you think, Molly?'

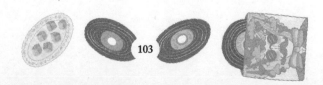

Beth was probably right – it would have been cool to hang out with Rita – but I *so* didn't want to spend any more time in a 1960 classroom, and lunchbreak was probably the best time for Beth and me to escape.

'Er … we're only meant to be here for a half-day today, remember, Beth?' I said. 'And we've got that thing … you know … that thing with Jeanie to sort out … so maybe …'

'Molly's right,' said Beth. 'Thanks, Rita, but we need to go now.'

'I'll walk you to the gate, and I'll save you a seat in Domestic Science tomorrow, shall I?' said Rita.

Now I felt really mean. What was Rita going to think when Beth and I failed to show up – ever again?

'Er, we might not be here tomorrow,' I said.

'Yeah,' said Beth. 'We're sort of trying out a few schools.'

'Oh,' said Rita, looking disappointed. 'I hope you choose this one. I think you'd love it – especially as it's so modern.'

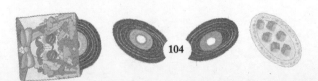

'It might not happen this year,' I said. 'But some-time in the future, we'll definitely be back.'

Beth and I followed Rita out the door and along the corridor. All the girls we passed were very quiet and polite – so quiet it didn't really feel like a proper school.

'Oh,' said Rita as she opened the front door. 'Mrs Gallagher is on gate duty.'

'Gate duty?' said Beth. 'I'm not sure I like the sound of that.'

'Oh, don't worry,' said Rita. 'Mrs Gallagher just stands there to make sure the wild girls don't sneak out to the shop to buy comics during lunchtime.'

What would Ruth say if she knew that twenty-first-century wild girls did worse things than sneaking out to buy comics?

'Anyway,' continued Ruth. 'You two have got per-mission to leave so ...'

I gulped. I so didn't want that scary teacher drag-ging Beth and me into the school for the second

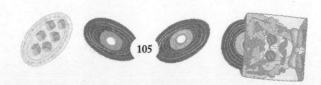

time that day.

What if she locked us up and we never got to escape?

'Er ...I think our parents might have talked to a different teacher,' I said. 'And Mrs Gallagher mightn't know that we're supposed to leave early.'

'And we wouldn't want to cause a scene or anything,' added Beth.

Rita looked confused for a second, and then she smiled.

'I can show you a place where it's easy to climb over the back wall,' she said. 'Mrs G will never see you there.'

'Know what, Rita?' I said. 'You're a star now, and you'll be a star in the future.'

Now Rita looked at me like I'd gone totally crazy, but she didn't say anything as she led us around the side of the building and showed us how to escape from school.

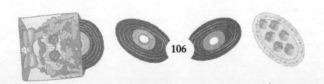

Chapter Eleven

Half an hour later Beth and I turned a corner and saw a sign: 'Orchard Road'.

'At last!' I said.

'But this can't be right,' said Beth. 'Where's the supermarket? And the phone shop? And the nail bar?'

She was right. Orchard Road is supposed to be part of the town – but this place was like a country road, with trees and fields and even a few sheep and cows.

'I guess a lot has changed since 1960,' I said.

The two of us walked along. It was totally weird, being in a place we should know so well, even though it felt like we'd never been there before. Finally we turned a bend and saw the familiar tall gates and red brick walls of Orchard House.

'Now what?' I asked. 'Do we have a plan?'

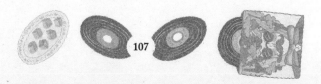

Before Beth could answer, we heard the 'squeak-squeak' sound of a badly oiled bike coming along the road.

'The plan is, we have *no* idea who's coming, so we hide,' I said, as I grabbed Beth and pulled her behind a large bush.

A second later, the 'squeak-squeak' was really close. Beth and I peeped through the leaves just in time to see a boy cycling through the gates. He was wearing shorts that looked like a man's suit with half the legs cut off, and a jumper that looked like it had been hand knitted in the dark. His hair was short at the back and slicked down in the front.

'OMG!' whispered Beth. 'Is that ...? Could it be ...?'

'It's Graham,' I said. 'Isn't he *adorable?*'

'He's totally adorable,' said Beth. 'And it looks like we're on time. I guess he's calling for Jeanie, so they can spend the day together. Wouldn't it be cool to hang out with them for a while? We could do all the things Graham said were such fun and we could give

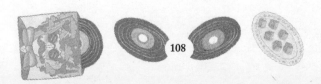

108

Jeanie a few warnings about climbing trees, and—'

'And it probably wouldn't make any difference,' I said. 'You're right, though. I guess we have to try. But quick – he's getting away. Let's follow him.'

* * *

Beth and I didn't want to walk on the noisy gravel, so we had to go the long way around on the grass. By the time we got near the back door, it looked like Graham had been there for a while. Beth and I ducked behind a tree and listened.

'Where's Jeanie?' whispered Beth. 'Why isn't she coming out?'

Then I heard the sound of a woman's voice.

'Jeanie is blind now. She is going to spend the rest of her life in an institution. NOW GO AWAY OR I WILL HAVE MY HUSBAND CALL THE POLICE.'

'Oh, no!' I said. 'We're too late. Graham told us

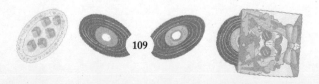

about this. It's Jeanie's mum blaming him for the accident.'

'Poor Graham,' said Beth. 'I get that she's worried about her kid and everything, but she still sounds like a crazy woman.'

We watched as Graham backed away from the door, and picked up his bike.

'I'm so sorry,' he said. 'I didn't know. I didn't mean to ... I'm sorry.'

But he was wasting his breath. Jeanie's mum had already slammed the door.

Beth and I watched as Graham slowly cycled away.

'Quick,' she said. 'We've got to follow him and tell him it's OK. We've got to tell him it's not his fault. If he talks to us now – or then – or whenever, maybe he'll get over it quicker. Maybe it won't ruin his life. Maybe he'll ...'

'So these two weird-looking randomers are going to hug him and tell him everything's going to be all right – and then everything will be all right?'

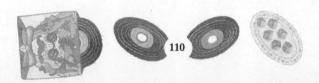

'Have you got a better idea?'

'Sure I have,' I said. 'A much better one.'

* * *

'Wasn't Mrs Gallagher scary enough for you?' said Beth, as we stood at the front door of Orchard House. 'Remind me again why we're taking on another crazy woman – it's like deliberately walking into a lion's den. Are you *sure* this is a good plan, Molly?'

'Of course I'm sure,' I said. (Now that we were actually there, I wasn't sure of anything any more – but I didn't want Beth knowing that.) 'If we talk to Jeanie's mum, and explain that none of this was really Graham's fault – maybe she'll let them get together when Jeanie gets out of hospital. Maybe Graham and Jeanie won't have to spend the rest of their lives apart.'

'But you said we can't change the past.'

'Well ... I *think* we can't – but I'm not really sure. Anyway, we won't really be changing the past – we'll

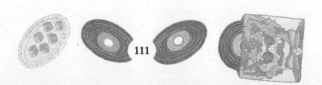

just be tweaking it a little bit.'

'You're right,' said Beth, as she reached up and pressed the bell. 'We have to try.'

A few seconds later we could hear the clickety-clack sound of high heels on tiles, and then the door opened. Beth and I took a step backwards – Jeanie's mum was tall and skinny and totally scary-looking. And then I noticed her red eyes and couldn't help feeling a little bit sorry for her. My mum went kind of crazy the time I broke my arm – and going blind had to be a million times worse than that.

'Hello,' said Jeanie's mum. 'Can I help you?'

'Er – we're friends of Jeanie's – from school,' said Beth.

'I'm Molly, and this is Beth,' I said, giving her my best smile.

Jeanie's mum stared at us coldly. (I guess my best smile wasn't good enough for her.) 'I haven't heard Jeanie mention your names before,' she said.

'Oh, that's because ... we've only been friendly

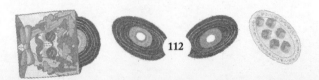

for a little while,' said Beth. 'But we're really good friends now.'

'Jeanie isn't here,' said her mother, reaching up to close the door.

'Oh, we know,' I said. 'We heard about her terrible accident – and we just wanted to see how she's doing.'

'And we heard about her not being able to see, and ...' said Beth.

Jeanie's mum interrupted her. 'She told you about her blindness?'

'Well, no,' I said. 'How could she? We haven't been to the hospital. We haven't even seen her since.....'

Beth nudged me and I stopped talking. If Jeanie hadn't told us about being blind, how were we supposed to know? This woman didn't look like she'd believe that we'd travelled all the way from the 21st century with the news.

Then Jeanie's mum gave a big sigh. 'Maybe you'd better come in,' she said.

Beth and I looked at each other. This *sooo* wasn't

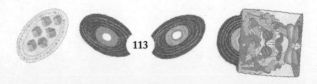

part of our plan – but if it was the only way to help
Graham ...

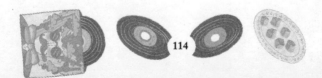

Chapter Twelve

'**Y**ou may call me Mrs Cottrell-Herbert,' she said as she led us into a very fancy living-room. I wondered what my friends' parents would say if I started calling them Mr and Mrs, but then I had to cover my mouth to stop myself laughing out loud when Beth did a mock-curtsey behind her back

We sat down on big flowery couches and about five seconds after Mrs Cottrell-Herbert rang the bell, the housekeeper came in.

'Tea for three please, Barbara,' said Mrs Cottrell-Herbert, and I felt like I'd wandered into Downton Abbey by accident.

The housekeeper went off, and Mrs Cottrell-Herbert stared at us for a minute. The only sounds were the ticking of a clock, and the faraway buzzing of an old-fashioned lawnmower. I felt like it was a competition to

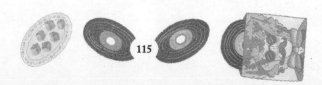

see who would crack first.

I sat on my hands so Mrs CH wouldn't see that they were shaking. Next to me, Beth was staring at a vase of dried flowers, like they were the most interesting things she'd ever seen. Just when I thought I couldn't take any more, Mrs CH started to talk.

'Jeanie has struggled to accept her condition,' she said.

'Well you can't blame her for that,' said Beth. 'It's only been a couple of ... ouch!' Beth stopped talking when I kicked her. The two of us had too many secrets, so I figured we'd do better by letting Mrs CH talk. Anyway, now that Mrs CH had started, she didn't seem to notice Beth's interruption – it was almost like she'd forgotten that we were even there.

'Jeanie has had plenty of time to get used to the idea of being blind,' said Mrs CH. 'It is unfortunate that she cannot accept her new situation.'

Now I felt really, really sorry for poor Jeanie. As far as I could figure, it was only a few days after her

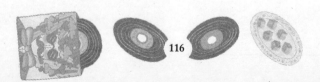

accident, and her mother expected her to be 'over it' already, like being blind wasn't really a big deal at all.

Just then the housekeeper came with the tea, and there was lots of faffing about with china cups and saucers and tea strainers and linen napkins that were so stiff I wondered if they'd be able to stand up on their own.

'So where was I?' asked Mrs CH when the house-keeper finally left.

'Er, you were telling us about Jeanie's ... blindness,' said Beth. 'But, Molly and I ... we ... well we wanted to talk to you about Graham.'

Mrs CH stared at me like I was an idiot. 'Graham? That boy who's been hanging around here during the holidays? Why on earth do you two girls want to talk about him? Do your parents need him to help in your gardens? He's a little rough around the edges, but he seems honest enough.'

'No,' I said quickly, wondering what Graham would say if he could hear this conversation. 'We don't want

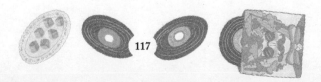

to give him a job. We want to talk about him and Jeanie. We thought maybe you were blaming him for Jeanie's blindness – and that so wouldn't be fair. Graham's really—'

Now Mrs CH actually laughed – but it was a cold laugh, like what she was laughing at wasn't the slightest bit funny.

'That's perfectly ridiculous,' she said. 'How on earth could Jeanie's blindness have anything to do with Graham?'

'Exactly!' I said, feeling relieved. Who knew this would be so easy? 'That's what Beth and I think too. Graham would never, ever do anything to hurt Jeanie.'

'I know they were together when Jeanie fell,' said Mrs CH. 'But that's not Graham's fault. Jeanie has always been wild and wilful. She has always been perfectly well able to get into trouble – and no boy could save her from herself.'

'But you were angry with Graham,' I said, hoping

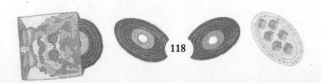

Mrs CH wouldn't wonder how I knew that.

'Perhaps that was unfair of me,' said Mrs CH. 'He caught me at a bad moment.'

'So maybe when Jeanie comes home from school for the holidays, Graham could come and see her?' said Beth.

'Absolutely not!' said Mrs CH.

'But you said—' I began.

'And Graham's so nice—' began Beth.

'Graham might well be nice,' said Mrs CH. 'A bit scruffy and common, but I'm sure he's a perfectly decent boy. I have to say he was always rather polite – for a town boy. And his father is a reliable hard-working man – once you get past the rough accent.'

'So why can't Graham—?' I began.

'Don't you understand, you silly girls?' said Mrs CH. 'Graham was never a suitable friend for a girl like Jeanie, but now ... well now that is no longer an issue.'

'How do you mean?' asked Beth.

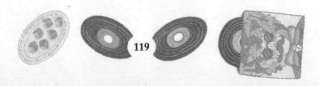

'Jeanie's life is different now. She can't be friends with you or Graham or anyone else from ... before.'

'But that's—'

Mrs CH interrupted me again. 'Jeanie is handicapped,' she said. 'She will spend the rest of her life in a home – being with normal people will be too upsetting for her.

'But Graham would never, ever do anything to upset Jeanie,' I said. 'He's a total sweetheart.'

'Sweetheart!' said Mrs CH. 'Show some respect! I would prefer if you would speak like a young lady rather than some ... vulgar American film star.'

'Er, sorry,' I said, even though I wasn't sorry at all. What's wrong with calling someone a sweetheart?

'In any case,' said Mrs CH. 'There is no room in Jeanie's life for "sweethearts". Spending time with that boy will only make her feel her loss more deeply – the loss of the life she used to dream of.'

Now I couldn't stop myself. 'So you're just going to keep them apart, and lock Jeanie up in an institution?'

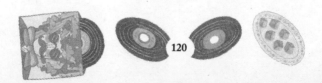

'Jeanie's doctors have given us no choice,' said Mrs CH. 'She will never see again, and it is cruel to expect her to survive in the outside world. In the end, we all have to face up to the hard truth.'

'But an institution? That sound so ...'

'It is a private school – the best place in the country,' said Mrs CH. 'There, Jeanie will meet people like herself. She will learn useful skills like basket-weaving and crochet.'

I thought of the wild, carefree girl that Graham had described. I tried to imagine her locked up in a darkened room, making stupid baskets that she'd never even be able to see.

'That's so not fair,' I said.

'Jeanie can still have a wonderful life,' said Beth. 'Blind people can run and cycle and ski. They can do all kinds of amazing things.'

'Haven't you ever heard of the Paralympics?' I asked, wondering if there was such a thing in 1960.

'You're talking nonsense,' said Mrs CH. 'And I

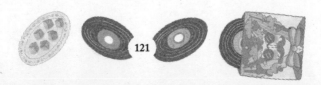

won't have it.'

'Jeanie's just blind,' I whispered. 'She's not dead. Please don't lock her away from the world.'

'It's cruel,' said Beth. 'If you love Jeanie, you won't do this.'

Now Mrs CH stood up. Her voice was icy. 'I think I will be the best judge of what's good for my daughter. This little chat is over. Good-bye.'

* * *

'Back so soon?' As usual, Rico didn't seem surprised to see us. I was beginning to wonder if anything could surprise that man. One day maybe Beth and I could trail back from the past dragging half the ancient Roman army, and a few Egyptian pharaohs behind us. Wonder what he'd have to say then?

'Thanks for letting us use your back door,' said Beth.

'My pleasure,' said Rico. 'Call back anytime – it's

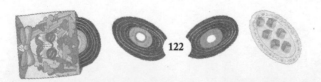

always delightful to see you.'

I *so* couldn't say the same about him, so I just gave him a fake smile and followed Beth out into the fresh air.

'OMG!' said Beth, as we walked down the alley-way. 'Just OMG!'

I knew what she meant. After travelling backwards and forwards in time, I felt like I'd been on the scariest roller-coaster ever. It was going to take a few minutes for my insides to stop spinning around in crazy circles.

We sat down on a bench and for a minute neither of us said anything.

'Poor Jeanie,' said Beth after a bit. 'I wish we could have changed the past. I wish we could have saved her from going blind.'

'Me too – and her mum is so horrible – imagine expecting Jeanie to be used to the idea of not being able to see after just a week or two?'

'Yeah, surely that would take years and years?'

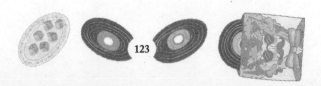

'I guess. It's good to know that Jeanie's parents didn't blame Graham but, in the end, that doesn't change anything really, does it? They're still going to lock poor Jeanie away – and they're not going to let Graham see her either.'

'We could tell Graham what we've found out, though. We could tell him that Jeanie's parents didn't blame him for the accident. When he hears that he can get on with the rest of his life without feeling guilty any more.'

'But that means we'll have to tell him about Rico, and the time-travelling and everything,' I said. 'I thought we were going to keep that a secret. We can't tell our friends because one of them is bound to talk about it at some stage. And we can't tell grown-ups because they'll get all stressed out about danger, and they'll have Rico's shop shut down on health and safety grounds.'

'Graham's not like the other grown-ups,' said Beth.

'That's so true, but …'

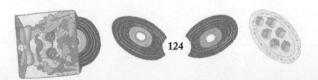

'I think Graham might be the only person in the whole world who we could trust with this secret.'

Suddenly I knew she was right. 'I agree,' I said. 'Let's tell him.'

'Do you think he'll believe us?'

'There's only one way to find out.'

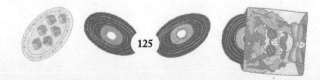

Chapter Thirteen

'So if Jeanie's parents didn't blame you for causing Jeanie's blindness, then Jeanie wouldn't have blamed you either. *No one* thinks it was your fault, Graham.'

'Beth's right,' I said. 'We went all the way back to 1960 so you won't have to feel guilty any more.'

It was half an hour later, and Beth and I were sitting on deckchairs in Graham's back garden.

'That's a charming story,' said Graham. 'And it's very sweet of you two girls to try to make me feel better. I'm lucky to have two lovely friends like you.'

'But it's *not* just a story,' I said. 'It's *real*. Rico is real and so is his shop.'

'We really went back to 1960,' said Beth. 'We saw Jeanie's mum. We spoke to her.'

'We even saw you,' I said. 'And you were so adorable

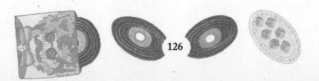

– all skinny and shy and trying to be brave.'

Graham laughed. 'You girls have such vivid imaginations – it must be because you read so much. Now who'd like to—?'

I jumped up so quickly my deckchair toppled over. 'We're *not* making this up!' I said.

'You're never going to believe us, are you?' said Beth.

Graham smiled. 'I like to think I am open to ideas, but time-travel – well it's a wonderful idea, but it has to be impossible.'

Now Beth jumped up too. 'My dad always says that seeing is believing.'

'And?' said Graham.

'So how would you like to come on a little journey with us? A little journey back to the 1960s?'

Whoa! This was moving *way* too fast for me.

Was Beth really suggesting that we bring Graham back in time?

That *so* wasn't part of the plan.

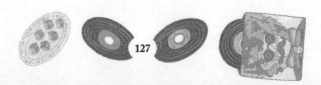

But Graham was already folding up the deckchairs and locking the back door.

'You're actually going to come with us?' I said.

'Your enthusiasm is infectious,' said Graham. 'And since I have no plans for the afternoon ...'

'OMG!' said Beth. 'This is so amazing. Do you actually believe us now?'

'I'm not quite sure I believe you,' he said. 'In fact, I have to tell you I'm struggling with the whole idea. But the world can be a funny old place – and I'm always up for an adventure. If you say you can take me back to 1960, it would be rude of me not to let you try. Now let's go before I change my mind.'

'Coming back to the past with us is great and everything, Graham,' I said. 'But what exactly do you think is going to happen when we get there?'

'Let's get there before we start to make plans,' he said. I knew then that he didn't really believe us. He was just going along with us so he wouldn't hurt our feelings. Graham might be the most fun grown up

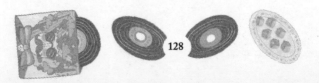

we knew – but he was still a grown up.

But Beth wasn't giving up. 'What would you like to happen when we get there, Graham? Do you want to meet Jeanie's mum, so she can tell you that she never blamed you for what happened to Jeanie?'

He thought for a minute. 'If this time-travel thing actually works ...'

'It *does* work,' said Beth.

'Well in that case, I have no desire to meet Jeanie's mum again. I've seen more than enough of her for one lifetime.'

'So what *do* you want?' asked Beth.

At first he didn't answer, and then all the words came out in a rush. 'In my wildest dreams – if there's any tiny possibility of going back to the time before the accident – if there's any possibility of seeing Jeanie herself – seeing her the way I remember her – that would be marvellous – oh how I would love to spend one single day with my dear old friend – the two of us roaming the fields the way we used to do. The two

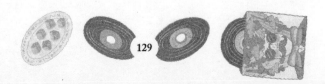

of us could laugh and joke and be so very, very happy.'

He smiled at us, and for a second, I didn't see his grey hair and wrinkles any more – all I could see was the sweet hopeful boy he had once been.

* * *

'Er ... hi again, Rico,' said Beth. 'This is our friend, Graham, and we were wondering if we could ...?'

Rico waved towards the curtain at the back of the shop. 'Everyone with an open mind is welcome,' he said.

'My mind is permanently open,' said Graham. 'But before we go, I wonder if you could explain.......'

'Explanations tend to muddy the waters,' said Rico. 'Just go. Experience. Have a nice time.'

'Hold my hand, Graham,' said Beth, as he followed us through the dark curtain. 'We *really* don't want to lose you back here.'

'Maybe you two can tell me how this works?' said

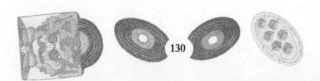

Graham. He sounded hopeful, like he really, really wanted it to work.

'Beth and I haven't exactly figured it out yet,' I said. 'We're kind of afraid to ask Rico any hard questions – but it's always sort of turned out right for us.'

'Yeah,' said Beth. 'How about you just think really hard about Orchard House and Jeanie, and hopefully we'll get back to where we need to be.'

'This is all quite ...' began Graham, but I couldn't hear any more as we stumbled forwards into the darkness.

* * *

We were on a bridge – a very big bridge over a very wide river in the middle of a city. The three of us stood on the footpath as old-fashioned bikes and cars and big, ugly buses streamed past us. Instead of traffic lights, there was a policeman standing on a platform in the middle of the road, using a white

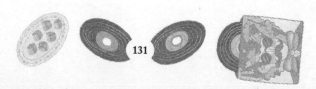

stick to direct the traffic.

'Where are we?' said Beth. 'This isn't our town or our river or our bridge. This isn't where we're meant to be. Where's Orchard Road, and Orchard House? Where's Jeanie? Maybe we should go back inside and ask Rico if ...?'

As she said the words, I turned around but there was no sign of the door to Rico's place.

'This makes no sense,' said Graham. 'No sense at all. What just happened, can't have happened. It's impossible.'

'Don't worry,' said Beth. 'The first journey through time is always the hardest.'

'Hey, Graham,' I said. 'Those weird cars are telling me that we've gone back to the past, but do you have any idea *where* we are?'

'I think we might be in ... Dublin,' said Graham. 'We're standing on O'Connell Bridge. This is really quite amazing. I don't know how you managed it girls, but you've made something very strange happen.'

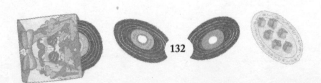

'But this can't be Dublin,' I said. 'Where's The Spire and the lovely restaurant mum brought us to for a treat last year? That should be just over—'

'I'm guessing The Spire isn't even built yet,' said Beth. 'And maybe the owner of that lovely restaurant hasn't been born.'

Graham was turning slowly around staring closely at everything. 'I often visited Dublin during the 1960's,' he said. 'Maybe the young me will come strolling along – I wouldn't mind seeing him again. There's a few things I'd like to say to him.'

'No,' I said. 'That *so* is a bad idea, Graham. Please don't make that happen.'

'I remember those buses,' he said, not really listening to me. 'And those cars – my dad had a maroon Anglia exactly like that one.'

'What's an Anglia?' I said.

'What's maroon?' said Beth.

Graham didn't answer either of us.

'But how can this possibly be ...?' he started to say.

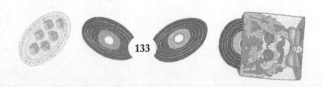

133

Just then a woman ran past us, leaving a trail of sweet orangey perfume in the air behind her.

'Aqua Manda,' sighed Graham. 'My sister's favourite perfume. I'd recognise it anywhere. She and her friends sprayed it on when they were going dancing – but that was all so long ago ...'

Graham had a dreamy look on his face, like he was half-asleep. I smiled to myself. Any other adult would be asking all kinds of hard questions by now, but Graham seemed to be accepting the impossible truth.

I pulled Beth's arm and we stepped a bit away from him.

'I know Graham looks kind of happy and everything,' I said. 'But what happens next? We've proved that we can go back in time, so maybe now Graham will believe us that Jeanie's mum told us she didn't blame him for the accident.'

'So you're saying we should go back home?'

'I don't think that's what I'm saying. Maybe we've

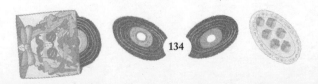

managed to get back to the time before Jeanie's accident? Maybe we should do what Graham wants, and find Jeanie before we leave? He so badly wants to spend a day with her – and maybe he can.'

'I'd so love to make that work for him.'

'Only problem is – we're in Dublin – miles away from home, and we still don't even know if we're in the right time. We could be years and years away from when we are meant to be.'

'I know this sounds kind of weird,' she said. 'But maybe we should trust Rico.'

'How do you mean?'

'Well, remember when we went back in time to look for my mum? Remember we decided it was like a quest, and we had to make a journey to prove we were worthy of getting what we wanted?'

'Yeah, but ...'

'Maybe we're meant to jump on one of these ugly old buses and find our way to Orchard House?'

I thought back to our trip to 1984. I remembered

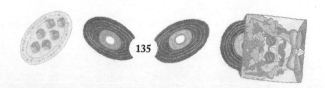

how badly Beth had wanted to see her mum. I also remembered how lonely, and hungry and afraid I'd been.

'A lot of that journey so wasn't fun,' I said.

'But it'll be different this time. Graham is with us, and he's travelled all over the world on his own. He's even been to the 1960s before. He'll take care of us. Come on, Molly, it'll be fun.'

'It will?'

Just then Graham came over to us.

'I don't suppose you can figure out what year it is?' I asked him.

He shook his head. 'That's such a bizarre question. I know what year it was when I woke up this morning, but now – now everything's topsy-turvy – and I'm not sure what to believe.'

'Look at the cars – and the clothes,' said Beth. 'Doesn't that give you a clue? Or maybe some of the buildings?'

'Of course,' he said, pointing to the air where the

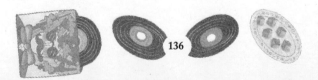

Spire should be. 'Why didn't I think of it before?'

'What?' I asked.

'Look over there, what do you see?' he asked.

'Nothing,' I said. 'There's nothing there.'

'Exactly. For many years there used to be a monument to Nelson there, but it was totally destroyed in an explosion.'

'When did that happen?' I asked.

'In 1966,' he said slowly. 'It happened in 1966.'

'So we're some time after 1966,' said Beth. 'I'm so sorry, Graham. We did our best but it looks like we didn't get here on time for you to meet Jeanie the way you remember her. That lovely summer you had with her had to be at least six years ago.'

'Maybe dreams aren't meant to come true,' said Graham sadly. 'I shouldn't have hoped for the impossible.'

A man was walking past with a newspaper under his arm. 'Could I see the front of that for one sec, please?' I asked.

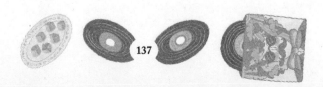

137

Instead of answering, the man unfolded the paper and held it out for me to see.

'Nine years,' I said, reading the date. 'It's 1969 and we're nine years too late.'

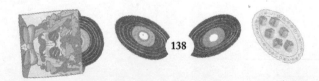

Chapter Fourteen

We found a quiet bench in a park and we sat there for ages.

'I'm sorry Graham,' said Beth. 'We trusted Rico and his stupid door. We really thought this would work. We really thought you'd get to spend some time with Jeanie.'

'And if that didn't work,' I said. 'If we arrived just after the accident, like Beth and I did earlier, we thought you could visit Jeanie in the hospital.'

'That would have been nice,' said Graham.

'And maybe seeing her and talking to her would have made you feel better,' I said. 'But now ...'

'Hey, Graham,' said Beth. 'I've had an idea. How old did you say Jeanie was when you last saw her?'

'She'd just had her thirteenth birthday.'

'And that was nine years ago – so she's twenty-two

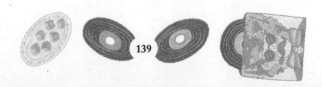

now – she's all grown up,' I said.

'But you can still find her,' said Beth.

'But she won't be …' began Graham.

I looked at his sad face, and for a second I could understand what was going on in his head.

'I know you wanted to relive the wonderful days you had with Jeanie when you were thirteen,' I said. 'And it doesn't look like that's going to happen now – but maybe …'

'… maybe this is the way things are meant to be,' said Beth. 'No offence, Graham, but if … er … old you showed up and tried to race around the fields with Jeanie, that might be a bit … weird?'

'I suppose you're right,' said Graham. 'I doubt I'd be able to keep up with her – and that would be hard to take. Maybe this way is best. This way we can find grown-up Jeanie and I can apol—'

'Graham!' said Beth.

'I know you keep saying I'm not guilty of anything,' said Graham. 'But I'd still like to tell Jeanie that I'm

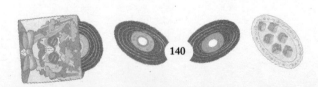

sorry for what happened to her – and for any part of it that might have been my fault. And I'd like to see if she's OK – if her life isn't too … grim.'

'That sounds fair enough,' I said. 'But how do we find her? You said her family moved away from Orchard House?'

'That's right,' said Graham. 'They moved a few months after Jeanie's accident.'

'Do you have any clue where they went – or where Jeanie lived when she was twenty-two?' asked Beth.

'I'm guessing it must have been around here some-where?' I said. 'Otherwise, Rico wouldn't have sent us here.'

'Jeanie might well have been in Dublin in 1969,' said Graham. 'But I have no way of knowing for sure. Maybe your phones that know everything can help?'

I took out my phone and looked at the screen. 'Sorry, Graham,' I said. 'Molly and I have been time-travelling for a while now. We're getting quite good, but our phones haven't got the hang of it yet.'

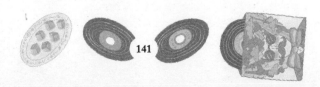

'How did you find out stuff in the olden days, Graham?' asked Beth.

'The library,' said Graham. 'The source of all knowledge in 1969.'

* * *

Graham led the way into a big grey room.

'This is a bit ...' began Beth.

'Shhhhhh!' said a very cross-looking librarian who was wearing a blue mini-skirt, white-eyeshadow and *huuuuuge* false eyelashes. 'Silence in the library.'

Graham went up to the counter and whispered loads of questions.

'Give me a few minutes,' whispered the librarian, smiling sweetly at him. I smiled too – even cross people can't be cross for long when Graham's around.

Ten minutes later the librarian came back with a big stack of books.

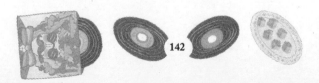

'I think you'll find everything you need here,' she whispered.

Beth and I followed Graham to a corner far away from everyone else, where it was safe to talk in quiet voices.

Graham opened the first book. 'What's that?' I asked, leaning over his shoulder. 'All I can see is a list of names and numbers – it has to be the most boring book in the world.'

'You girls!' said Graham. 'This is called a phone book – it's how we looked up peoples' phone numbers in the olden days.'

'Cool,' said Beth. 'How does it work?'

Graham gave a big sigh, and then he started to flip through the pages.

'It's alphabetical,' he said. 'Maybe we'll get lucky and find a number for Jeanie or her parents.'

He ran his finger down the lists of numbers and then closed the book. 'No luck here,' he said. 'There isn't a single entry for anyone called Cottrell or

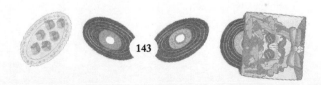

Cottrell-Herbert.'

'So what does that mean?' I asked.

'Jeanie's parents had many relatives in England, and I always suspected that they went to live there when they left Orchard House. The absence of a number for them seems to indicate that I was right.'

'But what about Jeanie?' I said. 'Does that mean she's not here either?'

'Not necessarily,' said Graham. 'She could be living here, but not have a phone. Her parents were wealthy so they always had one, but in 1969 that wasn't the norm. Most people managed to live perfectly happy lives without phones – hard for you two to believe, I know.'

'Wow!' said Beth. 'Unreal.'

'Anyway,' said Graham. 'Let's not give up just yet. Jeanie could very well still be in the country.'

'But how are we going to find her?' I asked. 'They *so* need Google around here.'

Graham patted the books and a cloud of dusk flew

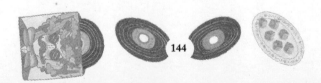

up into the warm air. 'I'm sure the information we need is in here,' he said. 'All we have to do is find it. Settle down girls, this might take a while.'

* * *

Graham slowly worked his way through all kinds of books – and finally he gave a little shout of joy. The cross librarian looked up from her desk with an evil look on her face, but when she saw Graham, she did a weird fluttery thing with her long eyelashes, and then went back to her work.

'What is it, Graham?' I asked. 'What did you find?'

'Look,' he said holding the book in front of me. 'It's a list of boarding schools for the handicapped in 1969.'

'You know you're not supposed to say "handicapped", don't you?' said Beth.

'Of course I do,' said Graham. 'And I would never hurt anyone's feelings by using a term they didn't like,

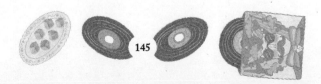

but in 1969 that was the only term we knew; I could
go through these books till the cows come home and
I'd never find a list of schools for visually-impaired
children or children with special educational needs.'

'I guess,' said Beth. 'How many schools for blind
kids are there anyway?'

'Just two in the whole country,' said Graham. 'So
it shouldn't be hard to figure out which one Jeanie
went to.'

'OMG, Beth,' I said. 'Remember what Jeanie's
mum said about the school?'

'Yes,' said Beth. 'She said Jeanie was being sent to
a private school – the best one in the country. Can
you tell if one of those schools is a fancy private one,
Graham?'

'You clever girls,' said Graham. 'One of the schools
looks like it's state-run and the other one is called
'Green Oaks Private School for Blind Girls'. I think
we might have found Jeanie's school.'

'But I don't get how that's going to help us,' I said.

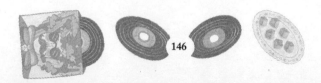

'Jeanie's twenty-two now. She couldn't still be in boarding school? Or could she?'

I had a sudden horrible picture of Jeanie growing older and older in the school, but never being allowed to leave. Were they going to keep her there, weaving baskets and crocheting shawls forever?

'I sincerely hope Jeanie left school a long time ago,' said Graham. 'But this is the best lead we've got.'

'How exactly?' asked Beth.

'Perhaps the school keeps track of their former pupils. There's a phone number here and if we ring them they might be able to tell us where Jeanie is now.'

'But our phones don't work,' said Beth. 'I keep checking mine, and it's totally useless.'

'Young people,' said Graham. 'So unimaginative. Now pass me that notepad and pencil please, Molly, and then we can go.'

Graham wrote down the phone number and we all went back to the library desk. He winked at the

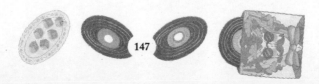

librarian as he handed the books over and she blushed all the way from her pointy forehead down to the high collar of her silky blouse. Then Beth, Graham and I set out into 1969.

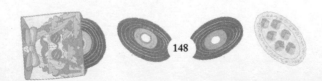

Chapter Fifteen

'You're sure all these people aren't on their way to fancy-dress parties?' said Beth when we got out onto the street.

I giggled. 'I know you lived through this time, Graham,' I said. 'And no offence or anything, but everyone looks really, really weird.'

'I was just starting to be a hippy in 1969,' sighed Graham.

'I've got news for you,' I said, I looking at his long hair and denim jeans. 'I'm not sure your hippy days are totally over.'

'Ah, if only you could have seen me then,' he said. 'Once I tie-dyed every one of my shirts and t-shirts. They were all ...'

'All what?' asked Beth.

'They were all a sludgy green colour. I could only

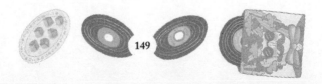

afford one packet of dye, and I fear it wasn't a great success.'

We walked past a huge ad for tennis racquets made of wood and then Graham stopped at a phone-box.

'I remember now,' said Beth. 'When Molly and I were in the 1980's ...'

'You know how bizarre that sounds coming from a girl who was born in the twenty-first century, who's currently hanging out in 1969?' said Graham.

'Yeah,' said Beth. 'It's weird all right! But anyway, when we were in the 80's we found money in a phone box and it pretty much saved our lives.'

I opened the door of the phone box and checked.

'No luck this time,' I said. 'I wish we'd saved some of that 1984 money.'

'That wouldn't help us anyway,' said Graham. 'In 1969 we had pounds and shillings and pence.'

'Never even heard of them,' said Beth.

'I remember it well, though,' said Graham 'There were twelve pennies in a shilling and twenty shillings

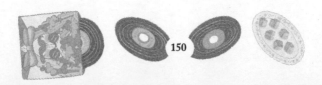

in a pound. We had threepenny coins and sixpenny coins and even halfpennies.'

'Maths must have been *soooo* hard back in the day,' I said.

'Enough about money already,' said Beth. 'All we need to know is that none of us has any – and we need to make a phone call. Anyone got any bright ideas?'

'When I was a boy I had a friend who knew how to make free calls by tapping on the receiver cradle,' said Graham.

'Don't look at me,' said Beth. 'I have *no* idea what a receiver cradle is.'

Graham looked up and down the street. 'And since my friend doesn't appear to be passing by right now, I think we'd better scratch that idea too. Looks like we'll have to move on to Plan C.'

'Which is?' asked Beth.

'Just watch,' said Graham. 'I hope I haven't lost my touch.'

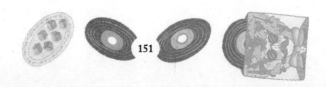

For a minute we stood there watching all the freaky people walking by. Then we saw a woman wearing a pale pink minidress with a matching pink coat and pink gloves and a pink hat that looked like she'd borrowed it from a jockey. Her lipstick was pale pink too – like she'd just been eating candyfloss and she'd forgotten to wipe her face.

As the woman came close, Graham stepped forwards.

'Please excuse me, madam,' he said. 'Perhaps you can help me and my young friends.'

For a second it looked like she was going to keep walking, but then Graham gave her one of his dazzling smiles, and she stopped.

'I have mislaid my wallet and I urgently need to make a phone call. I wonder if you could possibly …'

Before he'd even finished his sentence, the woman opened her funny pink cube-shaped handbag and pulled out a few coins.

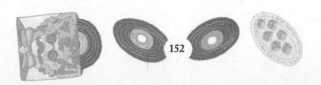

'Thank you very much,' said Graham. 'So kind of you.'

'Not at all,' said the woman. 'Happy to help.' Then she walked off with her pink high heels tip-tapping on the footpath.

I looked at the coins Graham handed me. 'Are you sure this is real money?' I asked turning the huge brown coins over in my hand. 'I mean I love the cute hens and chickens and all but ...'

'Trust me,' said Graham. 'It's real. I remember it well.'

'How much is this one worth?' I asked, holding up the biggest coin I'd ever seen.

'Hmmm,' said Graham. 'That's on old penny. I'm not exactly sure, but I think it might have been worth about a cent.'

'A cent!' I repeated. 'I guess you'd have needed a bucket full of them to buy a bar of chocolate.'

'Things were cheaper back then,' said Graham. 'And I could talk about that all day, but I'd much

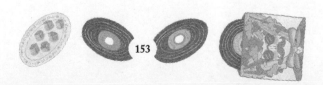

prefer to go ahead and make that call.'

The three of us squashed into the phone box, and Graham put some of the coins into the slot.

'What are these for?' asked Beth, pointing at two big buttons labeled 'A' and 'B.'

'If someone answers the phone, you push button A.' he said. 'But if there's no answer, you push button B and get your money back. Now stop distracting me please – I need to make this call.'

He took the paper with the number out of his pocket and picked up the receiver. Beth and I watched as he turned the dial for each number and then let it roll itself slowly back to the beginning. (Luckily phone numbers were short back in the day!)

'Quick, put it on speaker,' I said as he dialled the last number.

'Ha, no speaker in 1969,' he said. 'This'll have to do.'

He held the receiver towards us and no one said anything as we listened to the beep-beep sound of

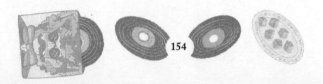

the phone ringing. After what felt like half an hour, the beeping stopped and we heard a woman's voice. 'Good morning. Green Oaks Private School for Blind Girls. Mrs Jenkins speaking.'

Graham pushed button A and there was lots of rattling as the coins dropped down.

'Hello,' said Graham, sounding posher than usual. 'So sorry for bothering you, but I am calling about one of your former pupils – Jeanie Cottrell-Herbert.'

'Ah, Jeanie,' said Mrs Jenkins. 'Such a charming girl – a little ray of sunshine – everyone here loved her. Now, how can I help you?'

'Well,' said Graham. 'Jeanie is a very dear old friend of mine, and I've lost touch with her. I was wondering if you could tell me where she went after she left your lovely establishment.'

'I cannot possibly divulge that sort of information.' Now Mrs Jenkins didn't sound so friendly. 'We have to respect the privacy of our girls.'

'Please,' said Graham. 'It's so very important for

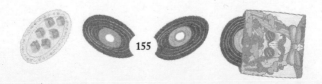

me to see Jeanie again.'

For a second all I could hear was the rumble of the noisy old buses going by and the voice of a newspaper man shouting something about a war in Vietnam.

'Please?' said Graham again. 'Please can you help me.'

I could see the beginnings of tears in his eyes, and maybe Mrs Jenkins could hear the change in his voice.

'All I can tell you is that we have a number of cottages in the grounds of our school,' she said.

'And did Jeanie move to one of those? Is she still ...?' Graham's posh voice was gone, and he sounded like a hopeful little kid.

'If I told you where Jeanie is, I would very likely lost my job.' said Mrs Jenkins. 'All I can say is that several of our former pupils live there. Now I really must go. Thank you for calling Green Oaks Private School for Blind Girls.'

'Goodbye – and thank you so very much,' said

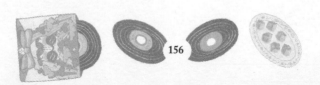

Graham as he hung up.

Then he turned to us. 'Do you girls think that Jeanie might be in one of those cottages?'

Beth and I laughed. 'Well, duh. Of course she is,' said Beth. 'Mrs J didn't want to break the rules, but she was definitely telling you where Jeanie was.'

'It's called a hint,' I said. 'A big fat hint. Now I love you two very much, but I think I've spent enough of my life squashed into this phone-box with you. Let's go – let's go find Jeanie.'

'But …' began Graham.

'It's perfect,' said Beth. 'We'll find Green Oaks school, and you can spend some time with your old friend. That'll be totally cool. And you can find out what Molly and I told you already – that it's not your fault that Jeanie's blind. Soon you'll be able to throw away all that guilt you've been dragging around with you since you were a little boy.'

'That sounds very nice indeed,' said Graham. 'But there's just one teeny-tiny little problem. Green Oaks

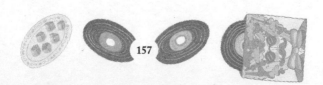

School is in Maynooth – and that's nearly twenty miles away – and we haven't got any money to pay for the bus.'

'Twenty miles is nothing,' said Beth. 'When Molly and I were in 1984 we—'

'No way!' I said. 'There's no way we're walking twenty miles.'

'Or we could—' said Beth.

'And we're not trying to trick our way onto a train or a bus either,' I said. 'We'll never get someone else to fall for our "electronic ticketing" story. All that stuff is much too scary for me. Why does Rico make things so hard for us? Why doesn't he ever land us right where we need to be?'

'I guess it's like when we went to look for my mum,' said Beth. 'It's sort of a quest – a mission.'

'But I don't like quests,' I said, blinking my eyes quickly so the others couldn't see the tears that were starting. 'Why does it have to be so hard?'

'It's not hard,' said Beth. 'It's fun!'

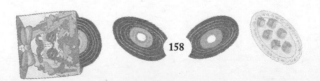

'That's not what you said when we nearly starved to death in 1984,' I said. 'We could have—'

'Now, now, girls,' said Graham. 'No point squabbling about the past – or the future or whatever 1984 is. Leave it to me. I think I have an idea.'

Chapter Sixteen

'You're *sure* this is a good idea?' said Beth.

'Sure I am,' said Graham. 'It'll work like a dream – I hope.'

We were standing outside a hairdressers shop. The front was painted in swirly patterns of mauve and purple, and looking at them made me feel a bit dizzy.

'Kevinz Kool Kutz,' I said. 'That's a really lame name.'

'Not in 1969, it wasn't' said Graham. 'Back then it was considered very fancy.

'And tell us again how you know Kevin,' said Beth.

'He was in my class at school,' said Graham. 'He never passed an exam in his life, and the teachers said he'd never amount to anything. He trained as a hairdresser and moved up here to open this place. It took a year or two to take off, but by 1975 he owned

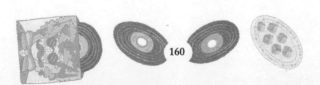

twenty branches of Kevinz Kool Kutz.'

'So how come we've never heard of them?' I asked.

Graham smiled. 'Kevin was a hippy at heart – and he was never comfortable with all the trappings of money and success. He sold the business and donated much of the proceeds to charity. Then he travelled to India, and set up a home for abandoned children.'

'Is he still there?' asked Beth.

'No. He died at the age of forty.'

'That's so sad,' said Beth.

'Indeed it is – but Kevin's was a brief, glorious life. He was the most generous person I ever knew – always ready to help all kinds of waifs and strays.'

'Reminds me of someone,' I said, looking at Graham, but he shook his head.

'Kevin was a better man than I could ever hope to be – that's why I'm so sure he'll help us. Now let's—'

'Hang on a sec, Graham,' I said. 'Don't forget, Kevin can't know the truth about who we are – and how we got here. I know you're nearly fifty years older

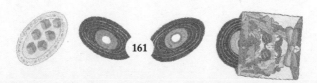

than you're supposed to be, but still, aren't you afraid he'll recognise you? Your face has probably changed a small bit, but maybe your voice?'

Graham smiled. 'Don't you worry about that,' he said. 'I've got a plan.'

* * *

Graham pushed open the door, and a bell jangled loudly. In the corner there was an old-fashioned record player, playing *Hey Jude*. (For a second I felt sad – that's one of my dad's favourite songs.) A man looked up from sweeping the floor. I blinked as I stared at him and started to wish that I was wearing sunglasses. He was wearing a tight purple polo-necked jumper and flared check trousers. Over the jumper he had a weird leather waistcoat with strings that swayed as he moved. On the waistcoat were loads of badges saying things like 'peace' and 'love' and 'flower power.' Wrapped over and over around

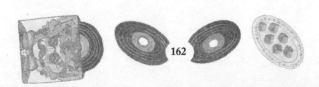

the neck of his jumper he had a long string of tiny beads in all kinds of bright colours.

'OMG!' I whispered. 'I think that might be one of The Beatles.'

'I'm guessing that's Kevin?' whispered Beth.

'That's him,' said Graham.

'Customers!' said Kevin. 'Three lovely customers. What can I do for you?'

'Och, we're tourists,' said Graham in a very bad fake Scottish accent.

Beth looked at me and rolled her eyes. I tried not to laugh. This was important – if Graham didn't manage to get money from Kevin, Beth was going to start talking about going for a very, very long walk.

'Dig your groovy threads,' said Kevin, looking at Beth and me.

I had no clue what he was trying to say, but Graham laughed. 'He means he likes your clothes,' he said.

I had to laugh. The words were so funny – and Beth and I were still wearing our school uniforms, which

are *so* not cool.

'Er ... I like your ... er ...' I was trying to be polite, but Kevin's clothes were so weird, I didn't know where to start.

'Your beads are lovely,' said Beth, helping me out.

Kevin smiled. 'They're love beads,' he said. 'All the rage in America these days.'

'Love beads,' I said. 'That's a great name. Are you supposed to give them to someone you love?'

'Not necessarily,' said Kevin. 'Love beads aren't just about love. They are also a symbol of peace and friendship. It's about communing with your fellow man.'

'Love beads,' sighed Graham. 'I *loved* love beads. I wore them around my neck and on both wrists. I gave them to nearly everyone I knew.'

I smiled. I could easily imagine Graham handing love beads out to random strangers passing him on the street. He wants to be friends with *everyone*.

Now Kevin put down his sweeping brush and was

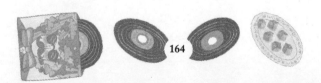

looking at Graham's long hair.

'I could do you a wonderful mop-top, sir,' he said. 'And you young ladies, how about a nice beehive hairdo for each of you?'

I had *no* idea what a beehive hairdo was and I was fairly sure I didn't want one.

'Och, you're very kind, so you are,' said Graham. 'But it's not haircuts we're after at all, at all, at all.'

I'm not an expert on accents, but I think his accent had taken a holiday from Scotland and ended up somewhere in Kerry.

Kevin was looking closely at him. 'You remind me of someone,' he said. 'But I can't work out who it is.'

'Och, I have a common face, so I do,' said Graham. 'The world is full of people who look like me.'

'Hmmm,' said Kevin, who didn't look convinced. 'Anyway, if you don't want haircuts, what can I do for you?'

'Well,' said Graham. 'I mean, och – myself and these two lovely lassies are visiting from Scotland –

and we need to get to our friend's house in Maynooth – but I've lost my wallet – and we were wondering if you have any jobs we can do – to cover the cost of the busfares.'

That sounded like a very dodgy story to me, not helped by the fact that Graham's accent sounded like it was going on a grand tour of Europe – but Kevin didn't seem to notice anything odd.

'You poor things,' he said. 'Of course I'll find something for you to do. Maybe you two girls could man the phone for a while?'

'But we're only thirteen,' said Beth. 'I'm not sure that ...'

'Oh, don't worry,' said Kevin, who didn't seem to notice that Beth didn't sound like she was from Scotland – or any of the other places Graham's accent had taken him to. 'The phone probably won't ring – it hardly ever hardly does. I've only been open for a few months, and I have to say business is very poor. I might have to consider closing down if ...'

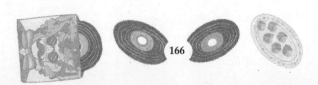

166

'But you can't close down,' I said, thinking of the twenty hairdressing salons that were in Kevin's future. 'Just keep going, and I'm fairly sure things will work out for you.'

'You should listen to Molly,' said Graham in a weird French accent. 'It's uncanny how that girl's brain works – it's almost as if she can see right into the future.'

'Let's hope she's right this time,' said Kevin. 'Anyway, I didn't catch your name.'

'Oh, I'm Grah—'

I had to kick him really hard. Kevin already half-recognised him, and if he said his name ...

'Grey?' said Kevin. 'That's an unusual name.'

'It's short for ... Grey Wolf,' said Graham. 'My parents read a lot of books about Native Americans. My little sister is called Shining Star and my brother ...'

Now Beth kicked him too. Graham was laying it on *way* too thick, and by now Kevin must have

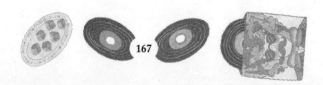

thought the three of us were crazy. Luckily Graham was right though, Kevin was a *really* nice man. He ignored all our weirdness and acted like it was perfectly normal for a man with a funny accent and two kids to wander into his salon, asking for jobs to make money for a bus-trip.

'I always have so much to do,' he said. 'I'm a lucky man that you three angels showed up when you did.'

* * *

For the next few hours, Beth and I sat next to the silent phone and looked at magazines full of brightly-coloured ads for weird things we'd never heard of.

'OMG!' said Beth, after a bit. 'Look at this, Molly. You can buy a screen to stick on your black and white tv so that it looks like colour.'

I looked at the picture she was holding in front of me. 'That's so lame,' I said. 'It's just a bit of plastic with blue at the top and green at the bottom. Everything

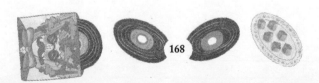

on TV will end up looking like a little kid's drawing. I'm so glad I don't really live in 1969.'

'Yeah, but you've got to admit that some of the jewellery's kind of cool,' she said, pointing at a picture of a woman wearing huge diamond-shaped yellow and pink earrings.

'I guess,' I said. 'And look at her eyelashes, I love the way they're so black and spiky – they make her eyes look huuuge.

'Twiggy,' said Kevin, looking over our shoulders.

'What's Twiggy,' I asked. 'Is that another word Beth and I don't know because ...?'

Kevin laughed. 'What planet have you two been living on?' he asked, pointing at the woman with the crazy earrings. 'That's Twiggy – one of the most famous women in the world. She was "the face of 1966", you know. Actually, with the right haircut, maybe one of you two girls could be the face of 1976.'

'That's OK, thanks,' said Beth. 'But I'm not going to be a model – I'm going to be a software developer.'

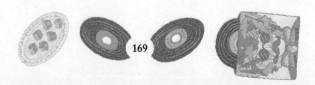

'What's a ...?' began Kevin, but then he stopped himself. 'I don't know where exactly you two girls are from, but it must be a million miles away from here.'

'It sort of is,' said Beth. 'I guess it sort of is.'

* * *

While Beth and I were busy not answering the phone, Graham cleaned out the small room where all the hair-dyes and shampoos were stored, and lined up all the bottles in alphabetical order.

After a while a customer came in, and Kevin welcomed her like she was a princess or something

'Give me an hour and I will have you looking like a film-star,' he said.

The woman started with beautiful, shiny hair, and when Kevin was finished, it was all puffed up like an ugly, furry football was stuck on her head. He held the mirror so she could see the back of her hair.

'What do you think of my creation?' he said.

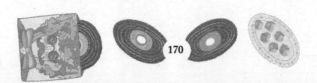

'Oh! Oh! Oh!' said the woman as she put her hands over her face. 'You've made me look like Dusty Springfield.'

'Poor Dusty Springfield – whoever that is,' whispered Beth. 'She's got a strange name and I'm guessing she's got totally strange hair too.'

'OMG!' I whispered back. 'No wonder the poor woman's crying. I'd totally *die* if I had to go out into the street looking like that.'

But then the woman jumped up from her seat and hugged Kevin and I could see that she hadn't been crying at all.

'I LOVE what you've done to my hair,' she said. 'This is the best day of my life. I'm going to tell all my friends to come here.'

'Weird,' whispered Beth. 'The 1960's are so, so weird.'

Next a man came in for a haircut and a shave. Kevin worked for ages, and then he stepped back, 'Ta-da,' he said. 'I think this is some of my best work.

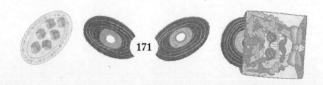

What do you think, everyone?'

'I think maybe Kevin needs glasses,' whispered Beth to me.

'Agreed,' I whispered back. 'He completely forgot to shave those clumps of hair on the side of the man's face. I get sideburns and everything, but this poor guy looks like he's got two fat black caterpillars crawling out of his ears.'

'They're having a race, to see who can get to his chin first,' said Beth.

'How's Kevin ever going to make his business work if he does stupid things like that?'

'You're right. If he goes on like this we won't make it to the end of his first year. You'll have to tell him, Moll.'

'Me! Why me?'

But suddenly Beth was very busy looking at the magazines, and Graham was still out the back. The customer was turning his head from side to side, like he couldn't make out what had happened. If I didn't

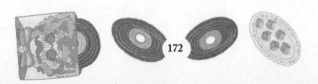

say it, *no one* was saying it.

'Er ... Kevin,' I said, pointing at the man's sideburns. 'Did you forget about ...?'

But the customer was smiling. 'This is so groovy,
Kevin,' he said, as he left. 'You've made me look like
one of The Monkees.'

Now I was totally confused. Monkeys are cute, and
I love seeing how they play with their babies and
stuff, but why would anyone want to look like one?

Just then Graham came out of the back room. 'Ah,
The Monkees!' he said. 'One of my favourite bands.'
The he opened his mouth and started to sing. '*Day-
dream believer and a homecoming queen ...*'

I don't want to mean, but Graham's good at lots of
things, and singing's not one of them.

I guess Kevin's ears must have been hurting too,
because he suddenly decided that we'd all done
enough work.

'You've been such a great help, you three,' he said.
(Which was kind of him, because Beth and I hadn't

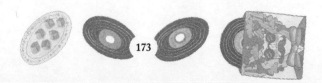

done a single thing.)

Then he went to the till and took out some money – probably all he'd made that day – and handed it to Graham. 'Here you go,' he said. 'More than enough to get you to Maynooth and back.'

Graham took the money and put it into the pocket of his jeans. 'Thank you so much,' he said in his normal voice. 'You are the kindest man .....'

He stopped talking and I could see tears in his eyes. I guess he knew he was never going to see his old friend again.

Now Kevin was staring at him. 'It's uncanny how familiar you seem to me,' he said. 'Are you sure we haven't met before?'

It was time to take action, before things got really awkward.

Beth grabbed Graham's arm and pulled him towards the door.

'If we don't leave now we're going to miss the bus,' I said. 'Thanks so much, Kevin – you've been a star.'

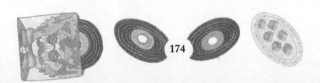

Then we opened the door, the bell jangled and we stepped out into the street.

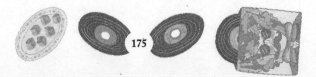

Chapter Seventeen

a few hours later, Beth, Graham and I were walking down the main street of Maynooth. We'd asked for directions, and knew that Green Oaks school was just at the edge of the town.

I was trying to be positive, reminding myself how well things had turned out when Beth met her mum in 1984. Part of me was really scared though – what if letting Graham meet Jeanie in her new, blind world was a really, really bad idea?

Maybe he'd feel guiltier than ever?

Maybe we were making a terrible, terrible mistake?

'Er ... Graham,' I said. 'I'm really hungry. Do you think we could use the rest of Kevin's money to get something to eat before ...?'

'I think that sounds like a wonderful idea,' said Graham. I guess he was scared too.

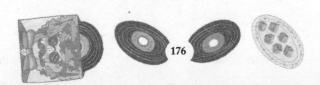

' The only restaurant we could find was called 'Murphy's Home Cooking.' Beth and I followed Graham inside and the smell of food made me realise that I was really, really hungry. A waitress in a black dress and a white apron showed us to a table in the corner of the room.

'Fancy!' said Beth, feeling the stiff white tablecloth.

'Not necessarily,' said Graham. 'It's 1969 remember. All restaurants are like this.'

The waitress came back holding a notebook and pencil. 'We've got bacon and cabbage or Irish stew,' she said.

I felt like crying. It was like the chef could read my mind and didn't like me and had picked the two dinners I hated most in the world.

'Have you got any wraps?' asked Graham.

The waitress shook her head. 'Never heard of them.'

'Bruschetta?'

'Never heard of it.'

'Pitta bread?'

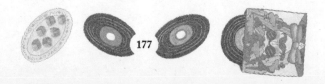

'Never heard of it.'

'Foccaccia?'

'Now you're just being rude.'

'It's 1969, remember,' I whispered to Graham. 'You've go to act like ...'

'Sorry,' said Graham. 'I keep forgetting. Remember I don't have as much experience as you two girls.'

The waitress was tapping her notebook with her pencil and staring at us like she hoped we were just part of a very bad dream.

'Maybe the nice lady could make us some sand-wiches?' said Graham.

The nice lady looked like making a few sandwiches was a very big deal, but then Graham smiled at her.

'Sandwiches for three?' she said, smiling back at him. 'Coming right up. We've got Easi-singles.'

'Or?' asked Graham.

'Or Easi-singles.' Her smile was fading a bit.

I'd been thinking a tuna melt or avocado toast, or a pulled pork bap, but I guess these weren't going to

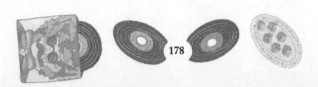

show up in Maynooth for another few decades.

'Sounds lovely,' I said. 'Thanks very much.'

* * *

We ate our sandwiches and washed them down with very strong tea, which came in a china teapot the size of a bucket.

I kept asking Graham to pour me more tea. I don't even like tea all that much, but the thought of what we had to do next was even worse.

Finally the teapot was drained and the waitress was circling the table like we were starting to annoy her.

'Time to go,' said Graham, and he paid the bill and Beth and I followed him outside.

* * *

None of us walked very fast, but even so, it was only a few minutes before we were standing outside a huge

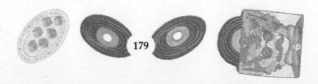

set of black gates. On the wall there was a sign:

Green Oaks Private School for Blind Girls

'Here we are,' said Graham.

I might have given him a hard time for stating the obvious, but that would've been mean. Just standing there was probably hard enough for him.

'I could have ... I should have ...' said Graham.

'You could have what?' asked Beth gently.

'I could have tracked her down,' said Graham. 'I could have found Jeanie, and spent time with her. We could have had all those years together – but I wasted them.'

'It's not your fault, Graham,' I said. 'You did your best. Jeanie's parents told you she didn't want to see you – and you respected that. You just don't know if they were telling the truth or not.'

'You're right,' he sighed. 'And in a few minutes – if I'm lucky, I'm going to see my Jeanie again.'

'So why are we still hanging around out here?' I said.

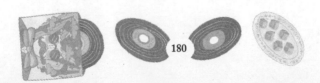

No one answered and no one moved.

The three of us stood on the footpath and looked through the gateway. Inside, there was a red-brick building that looked more like a fancy house than a boarding school. There were lots of trees and bushes, and hidden away at the farthest side of the grounds, we could just about see the roofs of a few small cottages.

'Where *is* everyone?' asked Beth. 'This has to be the quietest school I've ever seen.'

'Maybe everyone's inside having Latin lessons,' I said. 'Lucky them. Not.'

'Or maybe it's teatime,' said Beth. 'Maybe all the kids are inside stuffing their faces with Easi-Single sandwiches.'

'You've got to remember that it's the 1960s,' said Graham. 'Schools were strict back then.'

'Ha! I said. 'You don't have to tell Beth and me about that. We went to school in 1960, remember?'

'Well, then you understand what I'm trying to say,'

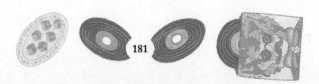

said Graham. 'In 1960s schools there wasn't much running around outside allowed – especially for girls. They were expected to spend much of their time indoors behaving like young ladies. That's why Jeanie and I ...'

He stopped talking and Beth patted his arm like he was a little kid. I stared at the red brick walls of the school and tried not to think too much about the girls inside. Were they all sitting in a dark room, making stupid baskets, and not allowed to talk or laugh or have fun ... or anything?

'Do we have a plan?' I asked.

'I guess we knock on the doors of the cottages until we find Jeanie?' said Graham.

'No offence, Graham,' said Beth. 'But that's not exactly the best plan I've ever heard. If we knock on a door and Jeanie opens it, that's great and everything, but what exactly are we going to say to her? How are we going to explain why three randomers are knock-ing on her door?'

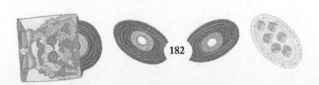

'I'm not a randomer!' said Graham. 'I'm her best friend.'

Suddenly I understood that Graham had forgotten an important detail. He might well have been Jeanie's best friend, but he was nearly seventy and she was only twenty-two.

'Sorry,' said Beth. 'We know that Jeanie's really special to you, but for now, you have to pretend to be a randomer, OK?'

'Beth's right,' I said. 'No matter what happens, you can't tell Jeanie who you are.'

'But how can I apologise to her, without telling her who I am?' asked Graham.

'We've been over and over this, Graham,' said Beth.

'And Beth and I even discussed it with Jeanie's mum,' I said.

'You don't *need* to apologise,' said Beth. 'You were a kid who suggested climbing a tree. Last time I checked, that wasn't a crime.'

'You may be right,' said Graham. 'But I've been

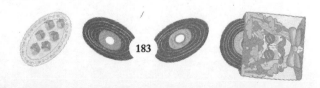

dragging this guilt around with me for more than fifty years – and now it's hard to let go. I need to talk to Jeanie – so she'll know that I didn't mean for her to get hurt.'

'I'm guessing she knows that already,' I said.

'Maybe she does,' said Graham. 'Maybe I'll be saying it more for my own good than hers. But in any case ...'

'I give up,' sighed Beth. 'I can tell you're not going to let this go. You're a smart man. I guess you can figure out a way to apologise, without exactly apologizing. But read my lips – DON'T TELL JEANIE WHO YOU ARE!'

'Yeah,' I said. 'It would totally freak her out.'

'OK, OK. I get it,' said Graham. 'And it's good to know that I'm in the company of time-travelling experts.'

'And, trust us, the first time is the hardest,' said Beth. I put my arm around her. I guessed she was thinking about the time she met her mum in 1984.

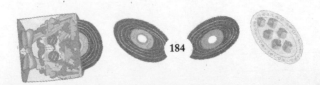

'So just take the lead from us,' she said. 'And it'll all be fine.'

'Well, it'll all be fine when we actually come up with a plan,' I said.

'The way I see it we've got two choices,' said Beth. 'We could stand here all day like idiots, or we can walk over to the cottages and see what happens.'

'That's a plan?' said Graham.

'It's the best one I can think of,' said Beth. 'Now are you coming or not? And remember, Graham – no funny accents!'

* * *

The grounds of the school were really quite cool – kind of like a secret garden with lots of pathways winding through the trees.

'Look at that huge tree,' I said. 'I'd really love to cl—'

I stopped myself just in time. Graham probably

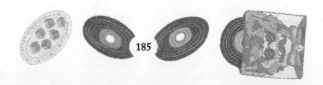

185

didn't want to think about climbing trees right now – or ever again.

No one said anything else as we slowly walked along the path. It was really peaceful. We couldn't hear the traffic any more, and the only sound was from a few birds singing at the very top of the trees.

Within a minute we were standing on a little patch of grass in front of three tiny, totally cute stone cottages. There were beds in front of each cottage, filled with masses of pink and red and yellow flowers.

'It's so beautiful,' whispered Beth.

'These are like houses from a fairy-tale,' I said.

I turned to look at Graham. I tried to imagine how he was feeling – he'd been waiting so many years to see Jeanie again, and now, for all we knew, only a few lumps of rock were keeping them apart.

'Graham, what do you—'

Before I could finish my sentence, we heard another voice.

'Hello? Is someone there?'

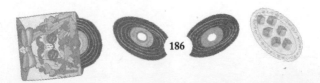

186

I was a bit creeped out, as I couldn't see anyone else, but without saying anything, Graham, Beth and I began to walk towards the voice. As we took a few steps forward, we could see a sunny terrace hidden away at the side of the farthest-away cottage.

On the terrace were pots of beautiful flowers.

Next to the flowerpots there was a pretty green bench.

Next to the bench was a very cute dog.

On the bench was a woman wearing dark glasses.

'Jeanie,' said Graham in a quiet, hoarse voice. 'It's Jeanie.'

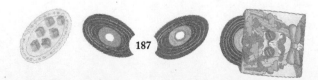

Chapter Eighteen

*a*s we walked closer, I began to shuffle my feet a bit on the gravel – Jeanie couldn't see us, and I didn't want to frighten her. The dog sat up and wagged his tail. Jeanie turned her head towards us.

'Hello?' she said again. 'Who is it?'

'It's ...' began Graham.

Was he going to break our rules in the very first second?

Was he going to ruin everything?

'Hi,' I said quickly. 'Sorry for disturbing you. My name's Molly, and this is my friend Beth, and Beth's uncle is here with us too. He's called ...'

I must know a million boys names, but for some reason, I couldn't think of a single one.

'He's called ... Darren,' said Beth. I rolled my eyes – there's a boy called Darren in our class and he's the

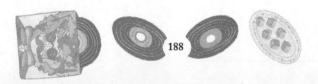

most annoying person I've ever met.

'Hi, Molly, Beth and Darren,' said Jeanie. 'My name's Jeanie, and this here is my dog. Her name's Blackie – don't you think it suits her?'

WHAT????

Blackie's an OK name for a dog, I guess. There was just one small problem – this particular dog was a beautiful golden brown colour, like caramel.

Poor Jeanie – she couldn't see the dog, and someone must have played a terrible trick on her. Should we tell her the truth, or ...?

Now Jeanie laughed, and for one second I could see the cute little girl from Graham's photograph. He'd been right about the way she laughed, it was a sweet sound that somehow made you feel better about the world.

'It's a joke,' she said. 'I've never seen Blackie, but I know she's not black.'

The rest of us laughed too. Right then I could see why Graham liked Jeanie so much. Being blind must

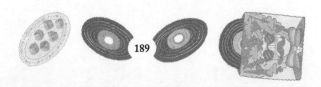

be really hard, but there was something so … alive about this girl.

'Can I help you?' she said then. 'Are you looking for someone?'

Oh, yes. We're looking for someone all right – and she's sitting right in front of us.

'Er – we were just out for a walk,' said Beth. 'And the gardens here looked so nice, we just kind of – wandered in. I hope that's OK?'

'Of course it's OK,' said Jeanie. 'It can be very quiet around here when the school is closed for the holidays. Would you like to sit down for a rest? It's very pleasant here in the sunshine.'

It was like a wicked witch had come along and put a spell on Graham. He was standing with his mouth half open, like a statue. It wasn't a good look, and, this might sound mean, but for a second I was kind of glad that Jeanie couldn't see him.

I had to feel sorry for Graham too, though. He's brave and old and adventurous, but still being back in

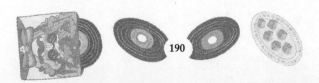

1969 was freaking him out. Sometimes I forget just how weird this while time travel thing is.

'Gr—'I began before realising my mistake.'I mean, Darren, would you like to sit here next to Jeanie? Beth and I don't mind sitting on the ground.'

'We totally LOVE sitting on the ground,' said Beth, as we made ourselves as comfortable as we could on the terrace.

Graham didn't move. Beth poked his knee. 'Darren,' she said. 'Jeanie's going to think you're weird if you just stand there.'

Like a zombie, Graham stepped forward and sat on the bench, about a metre away from Jeanie. He was all stiff and straight, like a shy kid on his first date.

What had made Beth and me think this was ever going to work?

Was this whole thing going to be a huge big embarrassment?

'Jeanie, is it OK if I stroke Blackie?' I asked. 'I get

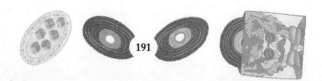

that she's a guide dog, and not exactly a pet – so if you don't want me to …'

'You know about guide dogs?' said Jeanie.

'Of course we do – why wouldn't we?' said Beth.

'Because Blackie's one of the first in Ireland.'

'She is?' I said.

'Yes,' said Jeanie, smiling. 'I could hardly believe my ears when I heard a story about guide dogs on the radio – and once I heard about them, I knew I had to have one. I had to go to England to get Blackie, and to train with her – we don't have a training unit here.'

Once again I'd forgotten that we were in 1969.

'But all that's going to change,' said Jeanie. 'A group of us is working very hard to set up a training facility here. Blackie has been wonderful, and I want all my blind friends to have the same opportunities as me.'

Graham was now acting like a sitting-down statue.

'Er … Darren,' I said. 'That's really interesting about the guide dogs, isn't it?'

'Yes,' he said in the end. 'It's fascinating.'

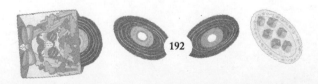

I held my breath. Was Jeanie going to recognise his voice?

But her face didn't change. I guess she hadn't heard his voice for nine years – and back then he was only a kid, and now he was old enough to be her grandad.

'There's something I need to say,' said Graham suddenly. 'I hope you don't mind, Jeanie, but it's been on my mind for many years, and I can't let it go. It haunts me all the time. I distract myself, and I travel whenever I can, but the guilt never goes away. When I was thirteen, I did a terrible, terrible ...'

OMG! Beth and I stared at each other – it was like watching a car crash. It was like the wicked witch had come back and put a new spell on Graham – one that made him talk too much.

What was Jeanie going to do if Graham just came out and said who he was and what he felt guilty about?

How could she ever, ever understand?

'Hang on a sec, Gr—Darren,' said Beth. 'We've just

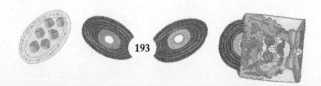

met Jeanie, and it's WAY too early for confessions.'

'So we just make small talk?' said Graham.

'Nothing wrong with small talk,' I said. 'It's much better than big, dangerous talk.' As I said the word 'dangerous' I stared at Graham, trying to make him understand.

'Do you mind if I ask you something, Jeanie?' said Beth then. (Beth's always been better than me at small talk.)

'Of course,' said Jeanie, smiling. 'Ask me anything – and I'll answer if it's not too hard.'

'It's just that most of the people around here are blind – so why are there so many flowers? Isn't it kind of a waste?'

'Not at all,' said Jeanie. 'There's so much more to flowers than the way they look. There's the scent, for one thing. And the way they feel.'

Without turning her head, she reached out one hand and stroked her fingers along the petals of a beautiful pink flower.

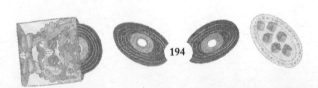

'And the flowers attract insects, which is a wonderful thing. Because the flowers are here, I can hear bees buzzing all day long.'

'No offence, Jeanie,' I said. 'But I didn't notice any of those things.'

'Neither did I – before,' said Jeanie. 'why don't you close your eyes for a moment?'

Even though she had no way of knowing what we were doing, we all did what she said.

'Now concentrate,' said Jeanie.

It took a minute, but she was right.

'Wow, that's like magic,' I said. 'I can smell something sweet and nutty – and I can hear the bees – I didn't notice them when I had my eyes open.'

'Now feel the petals,' said Jeanie. 'See how soft they are.'

Still with my eyes closed, I reached out my fingers to where I thought the flowers were.

'Ouch! Get off,' said Beth. 'You just stuck your finger in my eye.'

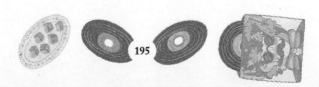

Everyone laughed.

'I guess it takes practice,' I said.

'Indeed it does,' said Jeanie. 'Indeed it does.'

This lesson about the five senses was all very interesting, but it wasn't really helping Graham. Suddenly I had an idea.

'Er, Jeanie,' I said. 'Do you mind if I ask you a question too?'

'Not at all,' said Jeanie. 'I like that you are so inquisitive. I hate the way children are told to sit down and be quiet all the time. What would you like to know?'

'You said you didn't notice things like the smell of flowers before, does that mean that you weren't always blind?'

'You're right,' said Jeanie. 'I wasn't always blind. I'll tell you what happened to me, if you like.'

Beth and I stared at Graham.

Was this story going to break his heart?

Or was it going to give him a way of saying sorry, without Jeanie copping on who he really was?

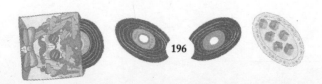

There was only one way of finding out.

Graham nodded. 'Yes,' he said. 'Please tell us what happened.'

'Of course,' said Jeanie, standing up. 'But first why don't I get us all some lemonade?'

'Would you like us to help you?' I asked. I had NO idea how a bind person could get into her house, and make drinks for us all.

'That's very kind, but Blackie and I can manage perfectly well,' said Jeanie.

She pulled Blackie's harness, and we watched as the dog carefully led her around the table and the flowerpots, and along the path towards the door of her home.

* * *

How do you feel, Graham?' asked Beth when Jeanie had gone inside. 'Is all this too hard for you?'

'I'm not sure how I feel,' he said. 'It's very, very

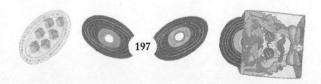

197

difficult, and yet it's wonderful too. I'm so happy to see Jeanie again, and I'm happy that she appears to be happy.'

'And is it OK that I asked her to tell us about her sight loss?' I said. 'I couldn't think of any other way to help you, so ...'

'You and Beth are two very sweet girls,' he said. 'Bringing me here, and staying with me while ...'

He stopped talking and I was really afraid he was going to cry, which would have been totally embarrassing.

'Let's close our eyes and smell the flowers again,' I said.

And that's what we did until we heard Jeanie coming back again. With one hand she was holding Blackie's harness, and in the other she had a very cool tray with a handle. On the tray there were four very full glasses of lemonade, and a plate of biscuits. Blackie led Jeanie towards us, and she put the tray on the table, almost as if she could see it.

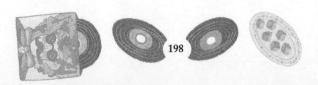

'I hope you like biscuits,' she said. 'I made a whole batch last night.'

'I never saw a biscuit I didn't like,' said Beth, and then we concentrated on the lemonade and the biscuits, until Jeanie said. 'You were asking about how I became blind.'

And Beth, Graham and I settled down to hear the sad story.

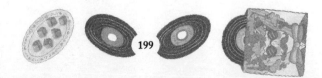

Chapter Nineteen

'I became blind during the summer of 1960,' said Jeanie. 'The last time I ever saw a flower, or a bird or the face of someone I love, I was only thirteen years old.'

'That's so sad,' I said. I looked at Beth and wondered how I'd live if I couldn't ever see her face again. What if I couldn't see my mum or my dad? What if I couldn't watch a hockey match, or draw a picture, or cycle my bike?

'Oh, Jeanie,' said Graham. 'I wish I could turn back time. I very much wish that I hadn't—'

Beth punched him in the arm.

'Shhh, Gr— Darren!' I said. 'Let Jeanie tell her story.'

'I had an accident that summer,' said Jeanie. 'I broke my arm in three places, and I had to spend a

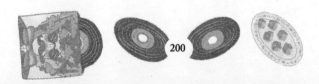

few weeks in hospital. I try not to have regrets, but it pains me a little that the last face I ever saw was that of the very strict matron – not a pleasant sight, I can assure you.'

Maybe there was some hope.

Maybe Jeanie had another accident in the hospital, and that was the one that made her blind?

'So you could still see after you fell out of the tree?' I asked.

'How did you know I fell out of a tree?' asked Jeanie.

'Oh,' I said, feeling like a total idiot. 'Lucky guess? I've been thinking about trees since there's so many lovely ones around here, and ...'

'Anyway, you're right,' said Jeanie. 'I *did* fall out of a tree. I climbed to the very top of the highest tree in our neighbourhood.'

'That was all my ...' Graham stopped talking when Beth punched him in the arm again. If he went on like this, he'd be black and blue before long.

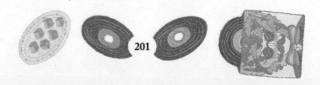

'But you could still see after you fell?' I said, hopefully. 'You said you saw the matron's face while you were in the hospital. Did you have another accident while you were there? Did you fall off a trolley or something?'

Jeanie laughed. 'I was a wild girl, but even I couldn't have two accidents in quick succession – and I was barely allowed out of bed while I was in hospital. The only danger I was in was the danger of dying of boredom.'

'So I guess after the fall, it took a while before you went blind?' said Beth.

'Yes,' said Jeanie. 'When I arrived at the hospital, I could still see shadows and outlines, but during those weeks I lost even that. By the time I left hospital I couldn't see anything at all.'

Now tears were rolling down Graham's face.

'Jeanie, I'm very, very sorry,' he said. 'So very, very sorry.'

Beth squeezed his arm. We both knew this was a

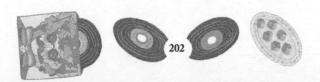

huge moment for Graham. At last, after all the years, he'd got the chance to apologise.

Jeanie must have noticed that his voice had changed. She reached over and touched his face. 'You're crying,' she said.

'I'm so sorry,' said Graham.

I wondered what she must have thought.

Who was this weird randomer who showed up out of nowhere and cared about something that had happened to her when she was a child?

Why was he crying?

And why was he saying sorry – over and over again?

But Jeanie was a nice girl, so she didn't say any of this.

'Going blind wasn't a walk in the park,' she said. 'But it wasn't quite as bad as it sounds. My parents had done their best, so I was as prepared as it is possible to be.'

'I don't get it,' I said. 'How could your parents prepare you?'

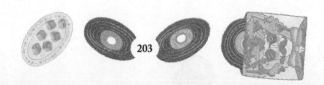

'I don't get that either,' said Beth. 'I know you said you were a wild child, but how could your parents have known you were going to fall out of a tree?'

Jeanie laughed. 'Nothing could have prepared me for falling out of a tree – that came as a complete surprise – and not one I'd ever want to repeat. But as for going blind – I'd known that was going to happen for many years.'

'You mean like you had a premonition or something?' I said. 'Or a crazy dream about the future?'

'No – nothing like that,' said Jeanie. 'What I mean is that when I was five, I was diagnosed with a progressive eye disease.'

'OMG!' I said, hardly able to believe what I'd just heard. 'You had an eye disease?'

'Yes,' said Jeanie. 'My parents told me all about it when I was seven – they thought it best for me to have some time to get used to the news. They explained that my eyesight would fail slowly at first, but in the end things would move quickly. Which was exactly

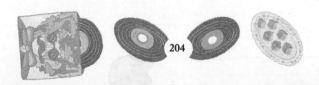

what happened. The doctors originally thought I'd be blind by the age of ten, so in a way I should be glad that I got an extra three years of sight.'

'So falling out of the tree didn't make you go blind?' said Beth.

'Absolutely not,' said Jeanie. 'The accident was an unfortunate co-incidence. I was going blind whether I fell out of the tree or not.'

I looked at Graham to see if he was happy. He was shaking a bit and his face had turned a grey-white colour like dirty sheets.

'OMG, Darren!' I said. 'Isn't that the best news ever? – I mean, Jeanie going blind is awfully sad and everything, but ...'

'I think what Molly's trying to say is that it's lucky you didn't go blind in a sudden accident, Jeanie,' said Beth. 'It's lucky you had some time to get used to the idea.'

'Yes, you're right about that,' said Jeanie. 'But even so, it wasn't easy, those years while my sight was

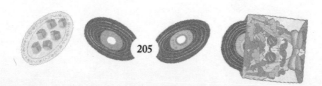

fading. I felt somehow – ashamed about what was happening to me.'

'You didn't have to feel ashamed,' said Beth. 'It was hardly your fault. You were just really, really unlucky.'

'I know that now,' said Jeanie. 'But back then, I was young, and I found it hard to face the truth. Some part of me believed that if I didn't acknowledge what was happening, I might escape my fate. I never breathed a word about my eye disease to any of my friends. I hid it from everyone.'

'That must have been lonely,' I said.

'It was,' said Jeanie. 'And the last summer, the summer of 1960, was the worst of all.'

'How come?' I asked.

'Well, in many ways it was the perfect summer. I spent most of it with my wonderful friend, Graham.'

Suddenly Graham jumped up. 'I hope you don't mind,' he said. 'But I need to stretch my legs.'

At first I thought that was really weird, but then I remembered my trip back to 1984. Back then, when

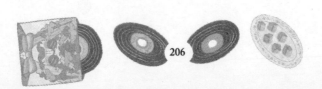

we were in the middle of some really intense stuff, Beth ran away to be on her own for a bit. Afterwards she told me that she thought her head was going to explode – maybe that's how Graham felt now.

Jeanie smiled in his direction. 'Maybe you could take Blackie for a little walk? She gets restless if we sit in one place for too long.'

'Excellent idea,' said Graham.

He took Blackie's harness and the two of them practically jogged along the path towards the school gates.

* * *

'I hope you don't think Darren was being rude,' said Beth. 'Sometimes he gets ...'

'... it's the long journey we had today,' I said. 'Darren always gets emotional when he's been travelling.'

'So you came a long way?' said Jeanie. 'That explains a lot.'

'Like what?' I asked.

'Well,' said Jeanie. 'You sound Irish – like me, but sometimes you say things and it sounds as if you've come here from another universe.'

I didn't like where this was going, but I could see Beth was *loving* it.

'Give me an example of something that sounds strange,' she said.

'You say this one thing and I've never heard it before,' said Jeanie. 'It's O.G.M. or G.M.O or something like that.'

'OMG,' said Beth, laughing. 'It's OMG. It means "Oh my God." I guess we do say it a lot – what else have you noticed about the way we talk?'

Now I was getting very nervous. How were we going to explain where our accents came from?

'I don't know if Jeanie's all that interested in the way we talk,' I said.

'Actually, it's fascinating,' said Jeanie. 'We can talk more about that later if you like. But first I promised

to tell you about my friend Graham.'

'Er, maybe Darren would like to hear that story too,' said Beth. 'Maybe you could save it for when he gets back from his walk.'

'Yeah,' I added. 'Why don't we talk about something else – except not weird stuff about things Beth and I say?'

Jeanie laughed. 'You two girls use the word "weird" a lot too, you know?'

'I guess we do,' said Beth. 'Hey, Jeanie, I hope you don't mind me asking, but what do you miss most, now that you can't see?'

'I don't mind you asking at all,' said Jeanie. 'I miss all kinds of odd things. For example, when Neil Armstrong walked on the moon a few weeks ago, I would very much have liked to be able to see the pictures on the television. I've heard the radio reports, but it's so hard to believe that it actually happened, don't you think?'

All I could think was that it was crazy that a man

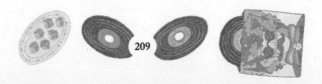

had just walked on the moon, wasn't that *ancient* history?

'What's that book you've got there?' I asked changing the subject. 'Is it any good?'

Jeanie reached out and picked up the book, which was on the table next to the tray. I guess when you're blind you've got to be *really* good at remembering where you put stuff.

'*Wuthering Heights*,' she said. 'It's one of my favourites.'

She opened the first page and ran her fingers along the raised dots.

'How does that work?' asked Beth.

'The dots represent letters,' said Jeanie. 'This one raised dot is "a" and these two dots here mean "b".'

'And three dots for "c" and four for "d"?' I said.

Jeanie laughed. 'It's not quite that simple. "C" is also two dots, but in a different position. In fact "e" and "i" and "k" are all represented by two dots in different positions.'

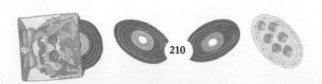

'That sounds totally confusing,' I said. 'I'm guessing it must take you half an hour to read a sentence.'

'Not at all,' said Jeanie. 'Like with most things, it gets easier with practice. Would you like me to read you a little bit?'

'Cool,' said Beth. 'We'd love that.'

'I'll read from the page I'm on,' said Jeanie.

She flipped the pages, until she came to a few sheets of folded paper, which she was using to mark her place. She put the papers on the table, ran her fingers along the page of her book and started to read. '... whatever our souls are made of, his and mine are the same ...'

'That's so romantic,' sighed Beth. 'I hope there's a happy ending.'

Just then a sudden gust of wind picked up Jeanie's bookmarks and they went flying towards the trees. Beth and I jumped up and raced around after them. Beth got the one that flew furthest away, and I picked up the others.

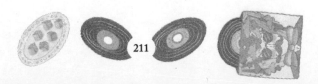

'Here you are,' I said, folding the pages I'd collected and holding them towards Jeanie.

'Hang on a sec,' said Beth running up with the last sheet of paper. 'What's on this page? It's really beautiful.'

'Don't ask me,' said Jeanie. 'Any page that's not written in braille is useless to me. They're just some old pages I found inside the last book I was reading. I've probably been using the same bookmarks for years.'

Beth held the paper towards me. It was a drawing of a bird – so realistic that it looked ready to fly right off the page.

'It's a bird,' I said to Jeanie. 'And it's stunning.'

Jeanie looked embarrassed. 'Oh, now I know what that is. Long ago, when I could still see, I loved drawing. I went through a phase of drawing every single bird I saw.'

'Wow!' I said. 'You were really talented.'

Then I felt bad. Was that a bit like saying 'you used

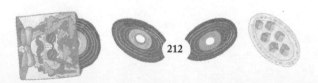

to be great at running' to some whose legs had just fallen off?

'That's very sweet of you,' said Jeanie. 'I presume the other pictures are of birds too?'

I unfolded the first page I was holding.

'Yup,' I said. 'This is a robin – and it's perfect. I think it's more real than the real thing. I want to stroke its wings and feel its little feet on my hand. And this next one's kind of green with a yellow stripe on its wing and on its tail.'

'A greenfinch,' said Jeanie quickly, even though she couldn't have seen one for nine years. 'One of my special favourites.'

'And the last one ... OMG!'

'What?' said Beth. 'What's wrong?'

I held the picture up so she could see.

'OMG!' she said. 'Just OMG!'

'OMG!' said Jeanie, laughing. 'Are you two girls all right?'

'Yes ... I think so,' I said. 'It's just that this picture ...'

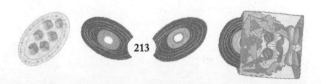

'Is it another bird?' asked Jeanie. 'I think I may have been a little obsessed when I was younger.'

No it's not a bird. It's a boy. A boy with huge dark eyes, and slicked back hair and a cheeky grin. A boy who used to be your very best friend, but is now an old man. An old man who can't tell you who he is, but who's gone walking around the gardens with your dog.

'No,' I said. 'It's not a bird. It's a boy. A very cute boy.'

'That must be Graham,' said Jeanie. 'He's the only boy I ever liked enough to draw a picture of. I was supposed to give him a present of it, but ...'

She stopped talking when we heard Blackie barking.

'Darren's coming back,' said Beth. 'Maybe you should fold up those papers again, Molly.'

I knew what she was saying. If Graham saw the drawing of him, he might totally lose it. And then I had the most amazing idea.

'Er ... Jeanie,' I said. 'This might be totally rude and everything, but I was wondering ... if you

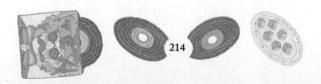

wouldn't mind … could Beth and I have that picture of Graham …?'

'I don't understand why you could want it,' said Jeanie.

'It's just that it reminds us of someone we know,' said Beth. 'And we think he'd really, really like to see it.'

'It would make him very, very happy,' I added.

'Well in that case,' said Jeanie. 'You can have it. You can have all of my drawings if you wish. They were precious to me when I could see them, but now they're just pages. All I need is something to hold my place in my book.'

'I've got something you could use,' I said, pulling the flyer for Kevz Kool Kutz out of my pocket and handing it to her.

Jeanie took the page and ran her fingers over it. 'I like the feel of this shiny paper,' she said. 'It's perfect.'

I picked up the drawings, folded them very carefully and put them into my pocket.

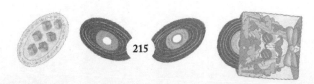

'Thank you so, so much, Jeanie,' I said. 'You'll never know what a kind thing you've done.'

Jeanie looked embarrassed for a second, and then she laughed as Blackie ran up to her, and licked her fingers.

'Hi everyone,' said Graham, who was a few steps behind the dog. 'I feel much better after my walk. Jeanie, you were going to tell us about the summer of 1960.'

'So I was,' said Jeanie. 'If you're all sitting comfortably, I'll begin.'

Chapter Twenty

'**I** spent most of the summer of 1960 with my best friend, Graham,' began Jeanie. 'I'd known him for quite a while by then. I attended boarding school, but as soon as the holidays came, Graham and I spent all of our time together.'

'So cute!' I said, like this was news to Beth and me.

'Graham and I first met when he came to help his father with some odd jobs in our garden,' said Jeanie. 'I confess that, in the beginning, I believed my parents when they said he was too rough for me – he was nothing like the sons of their friends. At first I let them persuade me to stay far away from him.'

'Ouch!' said Beth.

'Oh, don't feel too sorry for him,' said Jeanie. 'Graham wasn't very impressed with me either – I think perhaps he thought I was too posh for him.'

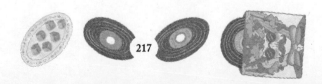

I looked at Graham who was nodding his head in agreement. He was smiling too, and it was easy to see that he was enjoying this trip back to his youth.

'But one afternoon Graham rescued a stray kitten from the top of our garage,' said Jeanie. 'And I could see what a gentle, kind person he was. The kitten was skinny and dirty and did its best to scratch Graham with its tiny claws, but still he held it like it was the most precious thing in the world. We brought it back to its mother … and … that's the day our friendship started.'

I smiled, as I remembered Graham's version of the story. Graham and Jeanie had rescued the kitten together – and while they were doing it, they both managed to see what a nice person the other one was. Who'd ever guess that a lost kitten could be so important in someone's life?

'How did you and Graham spend your time together?' asked Graham then. At first I was confused. He'd been there – he knew *exactly* how they

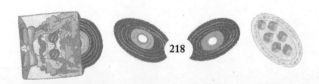

spent their time. But then I realised he was like a little kid who always wants the same bedtime story every night – something about how familiar the words are makes you feel all safe and warm and secure.

'Oh, we did all kinds of things,' said Jeanie. 'Swimming in the river, playing in the fields, having picnics.'

'Sounds you were living in the middle of an Enid Blyton book,' said Beth.

Jeanie laughed. 'Perhaps you're right – it *was* rather idyllic. Graham and I did other things too, of course. That last summer we used to dance to my favourite song – "The Twist".'

'Ah, "The Twist",' said Graham with a sigh.

'But then my father put a stop to "The Twist",' said Jeanie. 'I sulked for a while, but Graham said it didn't matter – he said the world was full of wonderful things we could do together.'

'That's so sweet, I said, looking at Graham, whose cheeks had turned pink.

'But as the weeks of that summer slipped by,' said

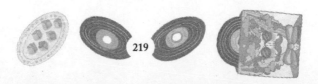

Jeanie. 'Things began to change ...'

She stopped talking for a minute. I remembered how Graham had said the exact same thing about that summer.

'This must be very boring for you,' said Jeanie suddenly. 'Why would you want to hear about that long ago summer?'

'No!' I said quickly. 'We love hearing stuff like this. Don't we guys?'

Beth and Graham nodded, which wasn't much good to Jeanie.

'What happened?' asked Beth gently. 'Why did things change?'

'I'd worn glasses ever since my eye disease was diagnosed,' said Jeanie. 'Every year I needed a stronger and stronger prescription – but that summer ... well, that summer my eyesight deteriorated quickly – and even with the strongest glasses available, I could barely see.'

Now it was all starting to make sense. I remem-

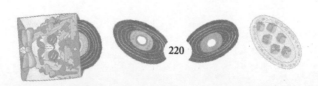

bered what Graham had said about Jeanie – how she stopped cycling and all the other fun stuff they did together – the poor girl couldn't see well enough to do any of it.

'That's why you stopped drawing.' Luckily Graham said the words so quietly that Jeanie didn't hear him.

'I did my best to hide what was happening to me,' said Jeanie. 'But, despite my best efforts, things had to change. I couldn't draw any more, cycling became impossible, and … well I couldn't run around like I used to do. I persisted in trying to live in a seeing world, when I could barely see anything at all.'

'That must have been so tough,' I said.

'It was,' said Jeanie. 'I still loved spending time with Graham – he was my favourite person in the world – and yet I hated being with him too. I knew he was confused. I knew he had no idea what was happening to me.'

'And what about your parents?' I asked. 'What did they say about all this?'

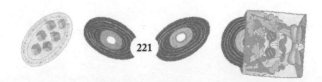

'For a while I was even able to fool them,' said Jeanie. 'I'd lived in Orchard House all my life, so getting around there presented no problem. And I made up excuses when I stumbled or dropped things.'

'Maybe your parents couldn't face up to the truth either,' I suggested.

'She smiled. 'I think you may well be right. I know now how hard this must have been for them.'

'You could have told Graham the truth?' said Beth. 'It sounds like he might have understood.'

'What clever girls you are!' said Jeanie. 'That's a good suggestion – but – I was very young. I was afraid that Graham would be disappointed in me. I was afraid he wouldn't want to spend time with me if he knew the truth.'

'No way!' said Graham. 'I never would have ... I mean, if you were my friend, I would have understood. I'd have found other ways to spend our time. We could have done all kinds of things together. I would have – I mean Graham would definitely have

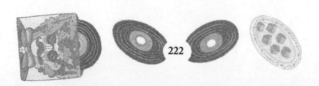

222

stood by you.'

Jeanie smiled. 'That reminds me of my favourite song – "Stand By Me". And I think you are right, Darren. Now I think Graham would have stood by me – and I'm sorry I didn't trust him enough to tell him the truth.'

Graham closed his eyes and sang the first few lines of 'Stand By Me'. When he sang the words about darkness and light and not being afraid, I thought I was going to cry – (and I barely noticed that he hadn't magically become a good singer).

When he finished singing, Jeanie turned towards him, like she was staring at him, which I knew was impossible.

'You're going to think I am very strange, Darren,' she said. 'I can tell by your voice that you're a bit older than me, and yet … there's something about you that reminds me of my old friend Graham … and that has to be impossible.'

OMG! Was it time for us to get up and run away?

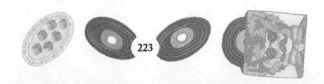

If Jeanie discovered the truth she might freak out.

But Graham didn't seem too worried. 'I'm sad to say that I'm a whole lot older than you, Jeanie,' he said. 'If you'd like to touch my face, you'll be able to see ... I mean understand that for yourself.'

'Despite what you see in the pictures,' said Jeanie. 'Blind people don't generally go around feeling the faces of strangers, but for some reason, you don't seem like a stranger, so if you don't mind ...?'

'Be my guest,' said Graham, sliding closer to her on the bench.

I could hardly breathe as I watched Jeanie raise both hands and rest her fingers gently on Graham's forehead, in the place where his hair probably started back in the day. Time seemed to stand still as Graham closed his eyes and Jeanie ran her fingertips along the wrinkled skin. She felt his long hair, which was hanging over his ears, and must have seemed old and coarse to her. Then she put her hands back on her lap. Graham still had his eyes closed, and for a

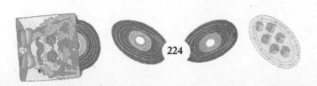

224

minute no one said anything. It was weird and crazy and very, very sad.

After a second, Graham opened his eyes and smiled. 'I always wanted a face massage,' he said. 'And I hope you weren't too disappointed, Jeanie, to find that I'm just a grizzled old man.'

Jeanie smiled too. 'I can tell that you're a little grizzled and very, very sweet.'

'Thank you,' said Graham.

I was starting to think that this might be a good moment to leave, when Jeanie started to talk again.

'I never met Graham again after that summer,' she said. 'He vanished from my life.'

That's because your parents chased him away, and now that you're older, he's too ashamed to face you because he has always thought that he was the one who caused your blindness.

'I missed him very much,' said Jeanie. 'But I think I can understand ...'

'I would never ...' began Graham before Beth

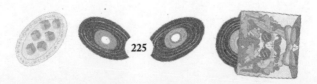

225

poked him in the arm.

'Maybe Graham tried to contact you,' I said quickly. 'Maybe he phoned you and called to your house and sent you letters and ...'

'My parents would have told me if he did,' said Jeanie.

'Are you so sure about that?' I asked, but then I noticed that Graham was shaking his head at me, and I realised that making Jeanie hate her parents wasn't going to help anyone.

'Maybe your parents thought that ...' I began, and then Jeanie interrupted me.

'I know my parents love me very much,' she said. 'When I went blind they tried to do their very best for me – but they couldn't understand what my life was going to be like. They thought they had to protect me. They thought that spending time with my old friends would make me feel even worse about what was happening to me.'

'That makes sense,' said Beth. 'Sort of.'

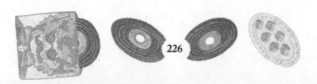

'Do you think Graham really might have tried to see me?' said Jeanie. 'I never once even thought of that.'

Now Graham spoke quietly. 'The way you described Graham, I feel like I know him. The person you described would have done anything in his power to be with you, to help you through what was happening to you. But I ... he was just a boy – a poor foolish boy who let the best thing that had ever happened to him slip away.'

Jeanie reached out and touched his hand. 'That's a very nice thing to say,' she said. 'Thank you.'

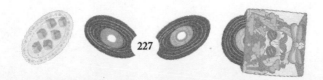

Chapter Twenty-One

The sun had moved away from the terrace and it was getting cold. My legs were stiff and I couldn't feel my bum any more after all that time sitting on the hard stones.

Jeanie stretched. 'This has been very nice,' she said. 'But soon my housemate will be home from work, and it's my turn to make the tea. We're having spaghetti – we just discovered it – but maybe you don't know what that is?'

'We've heard of it once or twice,' said Beth, laughing.

'Er ... do you go to work, Jeanie?' I asked, hoping she wasn't going to say that she sat around all the time waiting for time to pass, and for her housemate to come home. There's nothing wrong with making baskets, but if Jeanie said that's what she did all day,

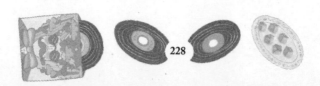

I think I'd cry.

'Oh, yes,' said Jeanie. 'Of course I've got a job. I'm a bus driver.'

'But …?' Was there a polite way to say what I wanted to say?

And then Jeanie started to laugh, and the rest of us joined in and we all laughed for a very long time.

'I have a wonderful job in an animal shelter,' said Jeanie, while Beth and I were still wiping the tears of laughter out of our eyes. 'Today is my day off. I answer the telephone, and feed the animals and care for them. I'm one of the lucky people who loves my work.'

'That sounds like a really cool job,' said Beth.

'It is,' said Jeanie. 'But there's more to life than work. I have good friends and a wonderful social life – a life my parents didn't dare to dream of for me. Sometimes I miss my drawing, but next month I'll be starting a night course in sculpture – so I can be creative again.'

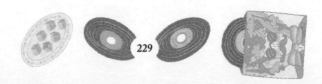

Suddenly I felt really weird. I was sitting in front of a very alive woman, and I was picturing the words from the death notice that wouldn't be written for nearly fifty years: *She will always be fondly remembered for her sculptures, which she donated to local parks, for the benefit of the community.*

'I bet you'll be really, really good at sculpture,' I said.

'I think Molly's right,' said Beth. 'And I think your parents were wrong. It sounds like you have a lovely life.'

'You're right,' said Jeanie. 'It *is* a lovely life – and I often think I have to thank my friend, Graham for it.'

'But I ...' said Graham. 'I mean he ... I mean you haven't seen him for nine years – not since you were a child.'

'You're right,' said Jeanie. 'But, in some ways, that doesn't matter. You see, I learned so much from being with him.'

'Such as?' asked Graham.

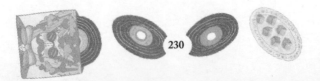

'Oh,' said Jeanie. 'It's hard to explain – my love of nature and music grew because of him – but it wasn't simply things like that. Graham made me believe I could do anything. According to him, I was going to be the greatest artist who ever lived. Of course that wasn't to be, but Graham's belief in me – well that made me believe in myself. I remember how he encouraged me to climb the highest tree, and—'

'Yeah, but you fell out of that tree and broke your arm,' said Beth. 'That so wasn't a good result.'

'Indeed I did fall out of that tree,' said Jeanie. 'But before I fell, those moments swaying at the top of the tree – well they were like magic. I could barely see the leaves and the fields below me, but I could feel the wind in my face, and the sun on my arms – and it was glorious. And because of that, I didn't go down the path my parents chose for me. I didn't lock myself away from the world and feel sorry for myself. I have lived – and I will continue to live as long as I am alive. And that's all due to my old friend, Graham. In

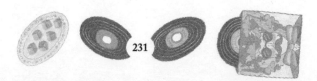

some ways, I have always felt that he's right next to me, standing by me.'

'That's so sweet,' said Beth.

'I don't expect to meet Graham again,' said Jeanie. 'But I know he's out there somewhere – and that is enough for me.'

Actually he's sitting a metre away from you with a totally soppy look on his face.

'I'm so happy things have turned out well for you,' said Graham.

'Thank you,' said Jeanie. 'This isn't Hollywood, so I won't pretend that going blind is the best thing that ever happened to me, but there have been some – compensations.'

'Like what?' asked Beth.

Jeanie thought for a minute. 'Now that I can't see, it's impossible to judge people by how they look. When you three wandered in here, I didn't form opinions about you based on your hair or your clothes.'

'That's lucky,' I said. 'Beth and I are wearing our

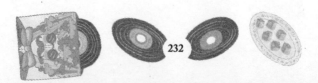

school uniforms and they so aren't cool. It would've been better if we'd been wearing our tracksuits.'

'Tracksuits?' said Jeanie.

'Just something that's popular where we come from,' said Beth quickly.

'Where *do* you come from?' asked Jeanie. 'You didn't say.'

Oh, we travelled many kilometres and many years to get here.

I had a funny feeling that Jeanie was going to start asking more and more awkward questions.

'I really think it might be time for us to go,' I said.

'Yeah,' said Beth, standing up and stretching. 'We need to get back home and your friend's spaghetti isn't going to cook itself.'

Graham didn't move. I felt so sorry for him – I guessed all he wanted was to spend a few more minutes with his old friend.

And then I had a wonderful idea.

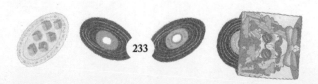

Chapter Twenty-Two

'Er, Jeanie,' I said. 'You know that song you and Graham loved – the one you used to dance to?'

'"The Twist"?' said Jeanie.

'Yeah, that's the one,' I said. 'Do you happen to have a way of listening to it?'

While I was asking the question, I looked at my phone to see if a miracle had happened and it was actually working. It wasn't though, and once again I wondered how people used to live without being able to use their phones for a million things every single day.

How did they listen to music?

How did they find their way around?

How did they do *anything*?

'Why are you so keen to hear "The Twist"?' asked Jeanie.

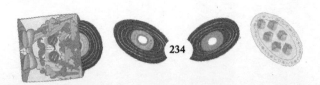

'We've never heard it before,' I said.

'But it's on the radio nearly every day,' said Jeanie.

'You girls have never heard "The Twist"?' said Graham. 'How have I let that happen?'

Jeanie stood up. 'I'm very lucky,' she said. 'I've got my own record player, and the first record I bought when I moved in here was "The Twist". Why don't I put it on?'

'Yesss!' said Beth and I together. Graham didn't say anything, but the look on his face made me think he was happy about it too.

Jeanie went inside, and a minute later, the sound of music came drifting out through the open door.

'Come on,' said Jeanie as Blackie led her onto the grass next to the patio. 'Let's do "The Twist".'

Graham jumped up and followed her and he and Jeanie started to dance. I've seen a lot of weird stuff in my day, but I've got to say that "The Twist" went straight into my top ten of weird. The music got going properly and Jeanie and Graham stood a bit

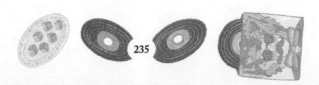

apart and did the craziest dance I've ever, ever seen.

They wiggled their hips and their knees, and every now and then they wiggled almost down to the ground and back up again.

'Come on, girls,' said Graham. 'Join in.'

Beth and I looked at each other.

'I guess,' said Beth in the end. 'No one we know's going to be born for years and years, so we'll probably get away with it.'

'And I'm guessing no one's going to film it and put it on YouTube either,' I said as I kicked off my shoes.

So Beth danced and I danced, and Graham danced and Jeanie danced and Blackie jumped up and down and barked like a crazy thing. And the song played over and over again, and after a bit, Graham moved over and held Jeanie's hand, and even though he's old and wrinkly and she was young and pretty, for those minutes it just seemed right.

Finally Graham went inside and turned off the music, and when he came back we all threw ourselves

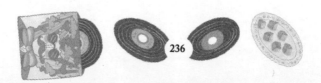

onto the grass and tried to catch our breath.

'OMG,' said Beth. 'You must have been really fit back in the olden— I mean now.'

Then Jeanie felt her watch and jumped up again. 'I am so sorry, everyone,' she said. 'This has been a very special afternoon – though I'm not sure why. But now I really must go take care of the tea. Come, Blackie – time to go inside.'

Graham looked really really sad, but he stood up anyway.

Beth grabbed my arm. 'Let's go, Moll,' she said. 'Why don't we wait for Graham over by those trees?'

So Beth and I thanked Jeanie for the lemonade and the biscuits and the music.

'You're welcome,' said Jeanie. 'It was my pleasure. Why don't you drop in again – I'm off work every Thursday?'

But I didn't want to think of Jeanie half-listening out for us every Thursday for the rest of her life.

'That would be totally great and everything,' I said.

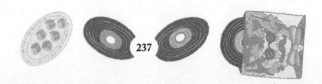

'But we live kind of far from here, so even though we'd love to see you …'

'I understand,' said Jeanie. 'Goodbye – and thank you.'

* * *

'OMG!' said Beth when we were safely over by the trees. 'I can't believe what just happened. Jeanie's blindness was nothing to do with Graham. She was going blind even if she never went anywhere near the stupid tree. Who'd ever have seen that one coming?'

'Not me, anyway! But don't you think this whole thing is a bit weird?'

'What's weird about time travelling?' she asked, laughing.

'Well of course time travelling's weird, but it's not just that.'

'So what are you saying?'

'Well, we really wanted to go back to the days

before Jeanie's accident – but we ended up here – where we thought we didn't want to be.'

'But still it all worked out,' said Beth. 'We got to see that Jeanie's happy – and now Graham doesn't have to feel guilty any more. It's almost like Rico knew exactly where to send us – like he had a plan – a much better plan than we had ourselves.'

'It's actually kind of cool,' I said. 'A bit scary, but very cool.'

I turned around and looked back towards Graham and Jeanie. They were standing by the cottage door, talking.

'I hope they're not too sad,' I said.

Then we heard Jeanie's beautiful laugh, and we both smiled.

A second later, Graham patted Blackie, gave Jeanie a quick hug, and walked towards us.

When he came close we could see tears in his eyes. That so wasn't part of the plan.

'Graham,' I said. 'I'm so sorry. Was this all a mis-

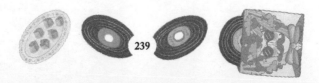

take? Maybe we shouldn't have... Maybe all this is too ...'

'Don't be silly,' he said. 'Was this afternoon difficult? Yes. Was it one of the best afternoons of my entire life? Also, yes. You two girls gave me a most precious opportunity, and I am more grateful than you could ever know.'

'So you're not sorry we came here?' asked Beth.

'Absolutely not,' said Graham. 'I always feared that I had ruined Jeanie's life forever – but today I have learned two things.'

'What are they?' I asked.

'I know that Jeanie's blindness wasn't my fault, and more importantly, I now know that her life is very far from ruined. That beautiful girl is happy – and that's all I need to know. Now can anyone remember where the bus stop is?'

* * *

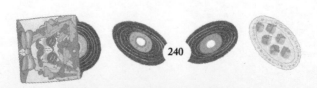

It was dark when we got back to Dublin, and finally found the emergency entrance to Rico's Store.

'Here we are,' I said. 'Let's go through quickly, before it vanishes again.'

'Get ready to say goodbye to 1969, Graham,' said Beth.

'Actually I've been thinking,' said Graham. 'I always loved the 1960's. I loved the music and the clothes, and—'

'Don't forget the love beads,' said Beth.

'And the love beads,' said Graham, smiling. 'I loved *everything*. In 1969 I was …' I had a horrible feeling I knew where this conversation was going. 'If I stayed here, Kevin would give me a job,' he continued. 'He wouldn't care that I'm not a youngster any more. And I could keep an eye on Jeanie – make sure she's OK – help her out with the things she can't do for herself any more. I could—'

Beth started to cry. 'That's such a crazy idea, Graham,' she sobbed. 'You can't stay here. Molly and

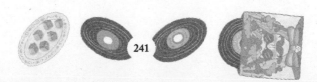

241

I would miss you too much. Dad would miss you too – and so would all of your friends. What about Charlie and Chang and … everyone?'

Now I wanted to cry too. '*Please* don't stay here, Graham,' I said.

'But—' he began.

'And we don't even know what would happen if you *did* stay,' I said. 'Would you just get older and older so that by the time you caught up with us you'd be … like a hundred and twenty or something? How's that supposed to work?'

'When Molly and I go back to the present, no time has passed,' said Beth. 'But if we go back, and you don't … we have no clue how that would turn out. It could be the biggest disaster ever.'

'And Rico mightn't let us back without you,' I said. 'And, no offence, Graham, but I so don't want to live in these crazy times. How would I even survive without my phone and my tablet … and my mum and dad?'

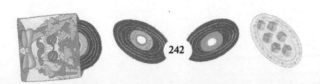

'Kids are supposed to love crazy ideas,' said Graham with a big sigh. 'Why do you two have to be so sensible?'

'Someone has to be sensible around here,' said Beth primly.

'I suppose you're right,' said Graham. 'I can't simply turn my back on the life I have, while trying to chase the dream of a life that was never meant to be.'

'I'm sorry, Graham,' I said. 'I wish things could have been different for you and Jeanie.'

He smiled at me. 'Thank you, Molly. Now are we going through that door, or are we hanging around here all night?'

Chapter Twenty-Three

'Graham's going to get such a great surprise,' said Beth. 'He's going to totally love his present.'

'You're right,' I said. 'I think it might actually be the best present in the history of the world.'

It was a few days later, and Beth and I were on our way to Graham's place with Jim and my mum. Mum was carrying a huge chocolate cake, Jim had a plate of chicken wraps, I had a bottle of lemonade and Beth was carrying the best present ever – the drawing of Graham that Jeanie had given us, now looking all fancy in a cool wooden frame.

'That's a great present, girls' said Jim. 'But you haven't forgotten Graham's little … oddity, have you?'

'Graham's odd in lots of ways,' said Beth. 'That's why we love him so much.'

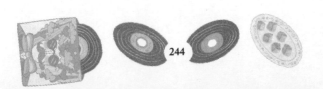

'True,' said Jim. 'But I'm just trying to prepare you for the fact that he probably won't hang that picture on his wall – and I wouldn't like you to be disappointed, after all your trouble.'

'Beth and I thought about that,' I said. 'But something makes us think that Graham will really, really like this present – and if he doesn't want to hang it up on the wall, that's OK too. The frame has a stand, so he can keep it on the table instead.'

'That drawing is so lovely,' said Mum. 'And it's exactly like the old photographs I've seen of Graham when he was little. But where exactly did you girls get it?'

'Oh,' I said. 'We—'

'We found it folded up in the pages of an ancient old book,' said Beth, smiling her best smile at Mum – the smile that always makes Mum forget to ask any more awkward questions.

'Well I have to say it's very thoughtful of you both,' said Mum. 'I'm sure Graham will love it. Now let's

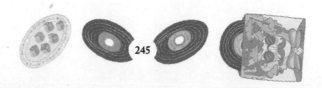

walk a bit faster, I think this chocolate might be melting.'

* * *

Graham's house isn't all that big, and it seemed like there were a million people packed inside. There were people in the kitchen and the living room and the hall. There were people sitting on the stairs, and even a few in the front garden. There were old people and young people and in-between people. I could hear about ten different languages. Some of Graham's guests looked like they were dressed up for the fanciest party ever, but others looked like they were headed to the beach. At the top of the stairs a man in a turban was playing a tune on what looked like a snake-charmer's pipe.

Mum and Jim took the food and lemonade into the kitchen. I could hear people admiring the chocolate cake, and Mum did that thing she always does

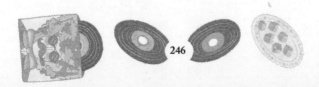

– 'Oh, it's nothing special,' she said. 'I just threw it together – and now I'm embarrassed I even brought it.'

Beth and I rolled our eyes and went into the living room.

'OMG!' said Beth. 'Just OMG!'

'I know,' I said. 'There's so many people here – but you're not surprised, are you? Graham's such a—'

'I'm not talking about the people,' she said. 'Look!'

And that's when I noticed. The walls of Graham's living room were covered with all kinds of weird and wonderful pictures. There were photographs from his albums, brightly-coloured abstract paintings that looked like things a toddler could draw, and posters of rock bands I'd never even heard of. Graham had gone from having no pictures at all – to having so many it looked like there had been an explosion in an art shop.

'OMG!' I said. 'What's happened here? It's like … I don't even know what it's like.'

'We've got to find Graham,' said Beth. 'We need to know what's going on here.'

I knew what she was thinking. We all love Graham for his eccentric ways, but now … had he actually gone and lost it completely?

Was this all our fault?

Beth and I had only been trying to help our friend, but maybe the whole trip to 1969 was a huge big mistake?

* * *

In the end we found Graham in the back garden, just finishing a chat with two women from the refugee support centre. They were talking about stuff that sounded really important, which was also really boring. Beth and I smiled and nodded for a bit, until the women decided to go back inside. 'I heard there's a wonderful chocolate cake,' we heard one of them saying as they got to the kitchen door.

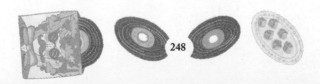

Beth and I hugged Graham. 'Happy birthday,' we said together.

'I guess you're twenty-one again,' I said. 'Like every single grown-up we know.'

'Not at all,' said Graham. 'I'm seventy years old and proud of it. It took a lot of hard work to get where I am, and I'm definitely not going to lie about it now that I've made it this far.'

I knew we might only have a few minutes of Graham to ourselves, so I got straight to the point.

'Can we ask you something, Graham?' I said.

'Of course you can. I am always ready to answer your questions,' he said, making me wonder if he was really a proper, paid-up member of the grown-ups club. Wasn't he supposed to make excuses and promise to talk to us later?

'Well, Beth and I … we've always wondered why you never had any pictures on your walls,' I said.

'And now that we've seen your walls today,' said Beth. 'Molly and I are wondering what's suddenly

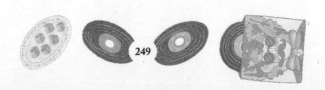

changed? How did you go from no pictures to a million pictures overnight?'

'That's actually two questions,' said Graham, smiling. 'But it's my birthday today, and I'm in a good mood – so I'm going to answer both of them.'

'You're *always* in a good mood,' I said. 'Well, nearly always, anyway. Will you answer my question first?'

'Well,' said Graham. 'Firstly, I'm surprised you actually noticed the lack of wall decorations in my home.'

I giggled. '*Everyone* noticed – but I guess we were all too polite to say anything.'

'Hmmm,' said Graham. 'Sometimes I wonder if people can be too polite. Anyway, in answer to your question, the reason for my picture-free state is Jeanie.'

'Jeanie?' Beth and I said the word together.

'Yes,' said Graham. 'You see, as you both know, I've spent most of my life filled with guilt because of Jeanie's blindness – and what I thought was my part

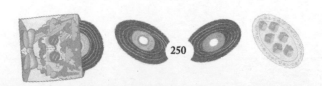

in causing it. That has affected me in many, many ways. So whenever I found a beautiful picture, my first thought was that Jeanie would never be able to see or to enjoy it.'

'That's so sweet,' said Beth. 'And so sad.'

'Maybe part of me even dreamed that one day Jeanie would visit my home,' said Graham. 'And if she did, I wanted to know that she would be able to enjoy it as much as I did. I made sure that all the nice things in my home could be experienced by touch or smell or sound or taste.'

'And that's why you never hung up any pictures,' I said. 'Even though you have heaps of ornaments – that Jeanie could feel with her hands.'

'Exactly,' said Graham.

'And now everything's changed,' said Beth. 'Now you know that Jeanie's blindness isn't your fault – you've turned your walls into, er … very colourful surfaces.'

'Well,' said Graham. 'You're half right. But there's

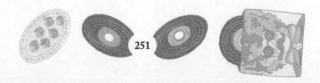

more to it than what you say. You see, after meeting Jeanie, I realised that even if I were guilty of hurting her, even then she wouldn't have wanted me to change my life because of that. She would have wanted me to enjoy everything – even things she could never experience again. Now I remember exactly how warm and generous that girl was – and I understand that I've been rather foolish.'

'You're so not a fool, said Beth, hugging him.

'Thank you, Beth,' said Graham. 'It might not surprise you girls to hear that I've been thinking a lot about Jeanie over the past few days – and I've come to understand a few things.'

'Like what?' I asked.

'Well,' said Graham. 'I wish I'd never lost her, but it's too late to change that now. Regret is useless. So I've been thinking more about the ways in which Jeanie changed my life. Losing her was hard, but it showed me how fleeting happiness can be. It showed me that I should grab life with both hands, and enjoy

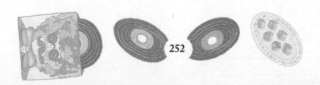

every single second of it. Thanks to Jeanie, I've had some wonderful experiences – and I like to think I've got a few adventures left in me too.'

'Yay!' I said. 'We need you to go back to China to pick up some more of that blooming tea – I so want more of that totally delicious vanilla and lemon one.'

'And there's something else too,' said Graham. 'I think that knowing Jeanie has made me more accepting of others.'

'How do you mean?' asked Beth.

'Well, Jeanie came from a very strict, narrow-minded family. When she was very young, she believed her parents' prejudiced views of other people, but as she grew towards her teens, she pulled away from that kind of thinking. She had a wonderful, refreshing openness to people. I like to think that ...'

'Judging by your party guests, I think Jeanie might have passed that on to you all right,' I said, as I looked back to the house, where a homeless man, two kids,

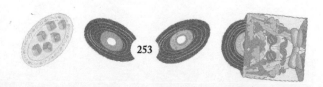

253

and the manager of the local bank were starting a conga line.

'Oh,' said Beth. 'Speaking of parties, we nearly forgot to give you your present.'

'You know your presence is present enough for me,' said Graham. 'But since you seem to have something wrapped up in that divine green and pink paper ...?'

We handed over the parcel and Graham ripped the paper off like an excited little kid. Then he held the picture and looked at it for a very long time. A few tears appeared at the corner of his eyes, and I hoped they were happy tears. Finally he wiped his eyes and gave us a huge smile.

'You wonderful, wonderful girls,' he said. 'I'm presuming you got this from Jeanie, and I'm not sure I even want to know what kind of story you told her first.'

'Oh,' said Beth. 'We just told her the truth. We said we knew someone who'd be very happy to see it – and I think maybe we were right.'

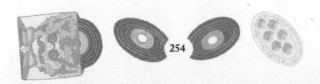

'You were so very right,' said Graham. 'I'll find a space on my wall and I'm going to hang this where I can see it every single day.'

'So it doesn't make you sad?' I asked.

'Absolutely not,' said Graham. 'I know I'll never see Jeanie again, but I'm a lucky man that I knew her once – and she will always be part of my life. Now why don't we go inside? I think it's time we showed those young people how to do The Twist.'

* * *

That evening, Mum and Jim said Beth and I could go out for an hour before bed.

'Where'll we go? I said as we went out the front door.

'We could go for milkshakes?' suggested Beth.

'That's a great—' Then I stopped. 'Actually there's something I want to do more than getting milkshakes.'

'*Yess!*' said Beth when I told her. 'Let's do that.'

So we went to the park and climbed up to the monument twenty times, and twenty times we rolled to the bottom of the hill, and we laughed till we cried, and some of the cool kids from our class saw us and we didn't even care.

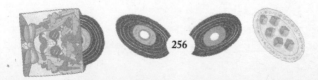